Ex Líbrís

Inside the Glasshouse

Inside
the
Glasshouse

GILES DIGGLE

faber and faber
LONDON · BOSTON

First published in 1990
by Faber and Faber Limited
3 Queen Square London WC1N 3AU

Photoset by Parker Typesetting Service Leicester
Printed in Great Britain by
Richard Clay Ltd Bungay Suffolk

A CIP record for this book is
available from the British Library

ISBN 0 571 14280 X

For Ann

Chapter 1

I was tempted to bunk off for the rest of the day. I was already over the fence and clear of the main building. I think I would have nicked off if it hadn't been so cold. No one would have seen me go. The terrapins and the incinerator block were in between me and the main building. There wasn't much vegetation to hide me at this time of the year, but I could have nipped along between the allotment sheds without being seen. No one was really interested anyway.

Now that I was on the other side of the fence I could run away, and I would have except for the cold and my desperate need to go to the bog. I was busting and that was why I was there in the first place. Hovis had got all the toilets covered.

The allotments were exposed and the wind whipped across them in February like nobody's business. I searched around desperately for somewhere to crouch down. I was sure someone would catch me in the act. Panic and the urgent messages from my bowels drove me down beside a large unkempt compost heap behind one of the dilapidated sheds.

It was an unpleasant business, but a relief. I didn't have any bog paper, so I had to make do and hope for the best. Hovis was a big enough problem without my stinking all the way through next lesson.

I had five minutes to get back. The cold and my timid nature drove me towards school.

School was a terrible place, a huge three-storey pile of rotting wood, concrete and glass. It looked as though it had been assembled by mental defectives using nothing more than old rugby posts, cracked paving stones and second-hand greenhouse glazing. We boiled in summer and froze in winter. Today was one of those rare days when the temperature seemed to be about right.

Beyond this old block was a new two-storey building, constructed in grey engineering brick. This recent addition to the school housed the Maths Department and all the practical, science and technology subjects. It was carpeted and more pleasant; the walls were painted in battleship greys and airforce blues. It was about five years old and had been imaginatively christened 'New Block', whereas the other parts of the school had risen from the dim mists of time. I had to get into New Block without meeting Hovis and the others.

I hopped out from behind the compost heap on to the allotment path and began walking casually back towards school. Beyond the fence I could hear a commotion, and a plume of smoke was rising from behind the incinerator, a sure sign that Arthur, the assistant caretaker, wasn't at his usual post, shovelling crisp packets and all our other rubbish into the fire. He'd sidled off somewhere to avoid the aggro at break. You couldn't blame him for hotfooting it to his cupboard or wherever he went when the bell rang and us lot came charging out of the block, smashing the doors behind us. If Arthur wasn't there, I'd have to avoid the incinerator. A lot of kids reckoned I was a creep, and if I went near them when they were smoking there would be trouble.

Instead of following the path to the incinerator, I cut across a ragged patch of sprouts and headed towards the far end of school near the bus stops, where some of the fence had been broken down with all the kids sitting on it.

I didn't get far though. I was half-way across the sprouts when a voice froze me in my tracks. I didn't dare look up. I clenched my teeth and pretended that I wasn't there. I walked along a little. The voice cut through the cold air again. It was Jacko calling from the incinerator. He was a fat, ugly kid in the same year as me, from 4H, the class next door to mine.

'Had a good crap?' he shouted. 'Scared to go to the bog, gayboy?'

I was flustered and tried to hurry on. I heard Jacko and his mate climbing over the fence. Now there was going to be trouble. My ears were burning. I tried to hurry on without running, to get to the gap in the fence and into the building before they could get hold of me, but I stumbled over a stalk which was bent over close to the ground under its burden of sprouts. By the time I'd picked myself up, Jacko was blowing smoke into my face. His little spotty mate Coomer grabbed hold of my collar and flicked his hot ash down the back of my neck.

'I reckon he's been having a toss, don't you, Jacko?'

Jacko smirked and sucked on his cigarette. Next, he'd take my glasses off. I'd been here before. Sure enough he grabbed them and passed them to Coomer, who chucked them into the broccoli.

'Well, come on, what have you been doing? Creeping up on us?' threatened Jacko, pulling me up by the collar and pressing his face into mine.

'No,' I said lamely. My eyes were watering and I couldn't see properly. I hoped Jacko wasn't thinking of sticking one on me.

Luckily the bell went and they sloped off towards school, but not before they'd sent me sprawling amongst the sprouts.

I groped around till I found my glasses and wiped the mud off the rims. I was late, so I ran as best I could, clambered over the fence, made my way round the main building and headed for New Block.

No one could say I was the best sprinter in the world. Just think of a hysterical chicken wearing spastic irons and that was me to a T. Everybody took the mickey out of the way I walked, so when I ran I was just laughable. They said I walked like a poofter, what with my knees knocking together all the time. I tried to straighten out my style, but somehow I couldn't get my legs going properly without my arms starting to do strange things. Also I was small and skinny, and the freckles didn't help. Mostly I got called a girl by the other kids.

'Piss off, Wayne, you girl,' they said.

'Girls line up over here!' the teacher used to say.

'Eh, Wayne, what are you doing over here with us?' the lads in my group would start shouting. Then they all fell about.

I was always getting shoved into the girls' toilets. It had happened ever since I was a little kid in the junior school. At fifteen it was all a bit much. 'Gaylord' was the name I hated the most.

I don't know what my mother was thinking of when she named me Wayne, Wayne Harding, after a dead cowboy actor. What sounds tough as a surname just doesn't work as a first name. I reckoned I must be a big disappointment to my mum.

Calling me a girl was not at all fair; I've never been in the least bit fanciable. No bloke would fancy a girl who looked like me. My brace didn't help, and it certainly made things worse for me when I got punched in the face. I got it caught in someone's scarf once going down the corridor, and it wasn't half painful. I got towed half-way

4

down to the Needlework Room before the girl even noticed, and then she didn't apologize. She was a Third Year, and all she could say was, 'Piss off, Wayne, I don't want my love bites going rusty!'

I felt that small. It was always the same: 'Wayne Harding doesn't go to the dentist, his mum takes him to the blacksmith's.' I had a mouth like a metalwork shop.

Fortunately, Jacko and his mate weren't in my Computer Studies option, so the story about me in the allotments wasn't going to get round for a while, and hopefully not at all. They'd probably find someone else to pick on by lunch-time and they'd forget about me for a little while. Anyway, I'd successfully avoided Hovis, and I hoped he was safely tucked up somewhere in his lesson. He wasn't in my option either.

When I got to the Computer Room, the class still hadn't been let in. Mr Crease was always late. He was another fat twit, a bit like Jacko, but more civilized. He was too pally with the kids to be a good Head of House. He was always late, or dashing off somewhere. Sometimes he stayed to teach us, but not often. Usually he let us in about ten minutes after the bell, wandered up and down a bit, and then left us to get on with our projects. Sometimes he didn't even bother to come back at the end of the lesson, and most of us thought this was all right because most of us liked to pack up early when they weren't playing games on the machines. Crease always had 'important' work to do elsewhere. Well, that's what he said.

I leant against a hot-air duct a little way down the corridor from the rest of the class, hoping I wouldn't get sucked into the conversation. If I could get next to Sharla and Becca it would be all right, but they were talking to Wilkes, and he and I didn't get on.

Wilkes was chewing gum and his earring glinted in a flashy, violent sort of way. He always talked about things he'd seen in videos, the sort of things which would make a normal person feel sick. Wilkes did nothing but watch TV, come to school to cause trouble and get drunk at weekends, or so it seemed from what he said. He talked a lot about sex, but I don't think he did much of that.

Crease arrived eventually. I noticed that as the year went on his beer belly had begun to stick out further from under his jumper. He was getting gross in his old age; all puffy-eyed under his glasses. His hair was an unreal blonde, revealing just a hint of black at the roots. It was dead shiny like a Cindy doll's, synthetic, as if it had been bought down the market and then ponced up a bit with hair oil. The girls hated him. He joked with them in a slimy sort of way and interviewed them alone in his room with the door shut. His room stank of talcum powder. He was creepy, they said.

The Computer Room was okay, except the blinds were always down so no one outside could see that Crease wasn't there, and if there was trouble no one could see that either.

There were enough machines for us to work one between two. None of the lads would work with me, and Wilkes always hogged a machine to himself. Anyone who argued got thumped. Crease couldn't handle him, so he always got away with it. Crease's way round the Wilkes problem was to put him in charge when he went out. He thought this would prevent trouble. It only made things worse.

I was always the one left without a machine, so I worked with Becca and Sharla, because they felt sorry for me. They weren't really my friends. I don't think they even liked me very much, and I never saw them outside school. I was just a lame dog to them, and they didn't like to see me being kicked.

It was nice to have someone to work with, but it did get a little boring, because they insisted on doing the project when Crease was out of the room instead of playing games like everyone else. I just had to go along with it if I wanted the company.

Nobody cared about their projects, except Sharla and Becca, because if Crease didn't give a toss about them why should they? Everybody knew that in the end Crease would fiddle the marks he sent off to the exam board, so there wasn't much point putting a lot of effort in.

After five minutes Crease left us alone as expected, and the hushed conversation was replaced by an electronic chorus of blipping and beeping. Wilkes and his mates took out their Walkmans and the room began to jangle and jingle like an amusement arcade.

I gave up on the stock-control program we were writing and let Becca and Sharla do it all. They didn't want my ideas anyway. They had soon tired of my suggestions and turned their backs to me. I swivelled my chair around and watched everybody else hunched over what they were doing, twitching and whooping at intervals. I longed to get my hands on the cursor keys.

This was okay until Wilkes glanced round and noticed me looking in his direction. Without taking his eyes off me, he stood up and began dancing around in the middle of the room, running his fingers through his hair and pouting until he'd got everybody's attention.

'Hey, there's a girl in here who fancies me!' he announced looking in my direction. Then he flicked his tongue around very fast in an obscene way like a hungry lizard. I didn't know what to do; I couldn't think of anything to say to defend myself. I wished I'd run away

7

when I had the opportunity. The blipping and bleeping died away completely. The silence was broken by Sharla.

'Leave him alone,' she said. Sharla Day was a small dumpy girl and not exactly pretty, but she was sharp, with a waspish tongue; she had the wit and the cruel streak necessary to deal with someone like Wilkes.

'Yer what?' he said, but with less certainty.

'I said, you should be so lucky, Wilkes. I mean who'd fancy you? I wouldn't want your scummy tongue flapping down my throat, thank you very much.'

'Oh, piss off!' shouted Wilkes, but he'd lost the battle and no one was interested in him any more. The blipping and beeping resumed.

'Thanks, Sharla,' I said, but I don't think she heard me. Sharla was again engrossed in her work with Becca. I turned round and pretended to work.

About fifteen minutes later, Stuart, a pimply kid from my class, put the lights out. Suzi Thomas screamed. Someone had made a grab for her; probably Wilkes. He was always groping girls. He couldn't borrow a pen without making a lunge. Wilkes was always finding excuses to borrow things. Wilkes thought every girl was a tart.

The lights stayed off. I couldn't tell what was going on. I didn't like the dark. The room glowed like Mission Control. I moved closer to Sharla and must have nudged her, because she screamed, 'Gerroff, Wayne!' and that got everybody cackling.

'Stick to boys your own age!' somebody shouted. I put my hands over my ears and didn't hear the rest.

That day was quite a good day. There'd been one or two tricky moments, but the cat-calling in Computer Studies eventually stopped. Crease came back five minutes before the bell, and I'd made it through to another lunch-time

8

without getting thumped. And I'd stayed clear of Hovis. School was always like this; daily I seemed to dice with death.

Lessons generally weren't too bad though. I wasn't particularly good at anything, but sometimes it was quite interesting. Between lessons things were considerably worse. Apart from anything else, there was the problem of getting from one end of the corridor to the other in one piece. There were few teachers about, which to you might seem like a good thing, but to me it could only spell trouble. I needed their protection. Things got totally out of hand. The corridors were dark and narrow because they ran along the north side of the building where the sun couldn't get in, and the lights never stayed on for very long. The stairs wound round precipitous stairwells, and were steep and slippery. The handrails wobbled dangerously when the crush between lessons descended or ascended, and threatened to collapse completely when traffic was pushing both ways. The pit at the bottom of each staircase was in total gloom and twice as narrow as the corridors. These pits were known as the Canyons. If you got jammed in one of them at lesson change there was little hope, what with kids running at the back of the crush and leaping on to the general scrum. It was difficult to stay on your feet, but you had to keep moving or be driven under. At best you'd get a sports bag wedged between your teeth. At worst Hovis would be lurking in a corner under the stairwell, like a malevolent octopus ready to strangle you before spitting out your remains into the swirling current.

What can I say about Hovis? He was out to get me. It was rumoured that he did unmentionable things to cats. Wilkes said so. He always made a big thing of it. Wilkes wasn't afraid of Hovis. Sometimes they were mates, but mostly they went their own ways, each protecting his own.

Hovis was dangerous; he was out of control. Hovis shouldn't have been at a normal school, because he was a loony. The teachers were sick of him, but they'd just given up. A lot of the time he got chucked out of lessons and handed over to the Deputy Head so he could look after him.

The trouble was, the Deputy Head was a drunk and didn't do anything. The rumours said he made his own booze on the premises. It started with beer, but now he'd gone over to the production of limited-edition whisky. His still was supposed to be installed in the darkroom in New Block. The door was always locked and no photography ever got done. No one respected him. Being sent to the Deputy Head was a soft option. Hovis would just get left in a room by himself, or be given the key to the Computer Room, while Mr Bottomly, our esteemed Deputy Head, a.k.a. Mustapha Crap, wandered off for a smoke in the VIP bog, which had been fitted out for the grand opening of New Block and was now reserved for school governors and important visitors. He spent more time in the bog than anywhere else. It was surprising he didn't interview parents in there.

Mustapha was never in his lessons, just like his mate Crease, so I was glad I didn't have him for anything. Hovis was in Mustapha's remedial set, so what with being chucked out a lot and then being left to Mustapha, Hovis just prowled about the building most of the time. Everybody'd given up complaining about it.

Hovis had got it in for me. I never knew why. He was twice the size of me, good-looking in a creepy sort of way, and he'd got muscles like knotted iron. His big handicap was that he was thick. He was pig-thick, but what was worse is he was twisted, completely off his trolley, much more of a maniac than Wilkes, who behaved like a choir-boy compared to him.

Hovis had always had it in for me ever since I had started at the school four years earlier. At first it was just name-calling, then arm-twisting and strangulations. In the second year he tried to extort money from me, but I didn't have any so he kicked me in on the way home a few times. I squealed, and he got thrown out of school for a couple of days. He laid off for a bit then, but started in on me again the year I'm talking about now. I told Crease, and I got kicked in again behind the Co-op and dumped in the big skip where they throw the cardboard boxes.

Crease said I had to grow up and fight my own battles, and then it wouldn't happen. That was okay in theory, but it wasn't all that easy if you were small, irritating, and looked like me. So I just tried to stay away from Hovis. I ducked and dived around the building like a hunted animal.

Chapter 2

I survived that Tuesday lunch-time by sneaking straight up to the Resources Centre after Computer Studies. I could hide there in relative safety on Tuesdays and Thursdays, because that was when our year were allowed in, and Hovis was banned.

I sneaked bits of sandwich from my lunch-box as I pretended to browse round the shelves. The place was always crowded with kids who came in to keep out of the cold, or hide like me from the less pleasant aspects of school life. As far as I was concerned, this lunch-time wasn't long enough, and all too soon the afternoon bell was beckoning me towards further torture.

Registration was pandemonium as usual, with kids running across desks and chucking things about. Mrs Roberts, our form tutor, had a tendency to linger in the staffroom and then arrive at the last minute to check our attendance, though how she did it with us all moving around I don't know. I can't blame her for coming late, because we were a pretty ugly lot and if I was her I wouldn't have come at all. When she finally turned up she shouted at us, her voice a mere whisper against the demented throng, and nobody listened. As the bell went, we rushed out of the room leaving a confusion of furniture behind. The room was no beauty spot to begin with, but day by day we were destroying it, together with the unfortunate Mrs Roberts.

Hovis liked Games, and always got there early, so I

hung about a bit in one of the porches in the main block to observe the queue forming outside the changing rooms opposite. When I saw it begin to move, I cut across the yard and joined the end of the line. Mr Rimbold stood at the doorjamb to watch us go in. Rimbold didn't put up with any messing about. He'd been teaching at the school a long time and was always moaning about how it had changed for the worse. He was getting on a bit and was more interested in flogging sports equipment than he was in teaching us PE. Rimbold kept going on and on about early retirement and setting up his own shop. He had about as much chance of doing that as I had of decking Hovis.

In the summer term, Hovis visualized me as a set of stumps and hurled cricket balls at me. In the winter months I was his football, and whenever we had Gym I became his human punch-bag. Rimbold couldn't, or wouldn't, keep his eye on everything. Hovis took any opportunity to bloody me in the 'finer aspects of contact sports' as Rimbold referred to them in his more light-hearted moments.

Once I'd got into the changing rooms, I chose a peg near to Rimbold's office, because that was generally the safest thing to do. No sooner had I started to unbutton my shirt than Hovis plonked his flashy sports bag down on the bench next to me. Rimbold had shut the door of his office to make a phone call. Doing a deal in training shoes no doubt.

'How's my favourite gayboy then?' said Hovis as he sat down next to me. 'Mind if I sit here, Twiggy?'

I was in no position to argue.

'Don't mind,' I said noncommittally.

'Been to Tesco's?' There was a nasty sneer in his voice as he picked my carrier bag up off the floor and started to pull out my sports kit.

'Give it back,' I shouted, trying to snatch it off him, but he whipped it out of reach and dangled it over my head.

'What's up? I'm only looking,' he said in that ugly voice of his.

Nobody else was taking any notice. Everyone was changing noisily, minding their own business.

Hovis threw everything on to the floor, item by miserable item, and ground each one under his heel like he was stubbing out cigarettes.

At that moment, Rimbold came out of his office and shouted, 'Valuables for safe-keeping! Bring them up to me!'

As the first boys moved forward to deposit their watches in the box, he uttered the word which made my heart sink: 'Trainers!' This was a sign either that he was in a lazy mood, having eaten too heartily at lunch-time, or else that he had to follow up whatever deal it was he had been cooking on the phone. Whichever way, it meant he was going to inflict the cross-country course on us.

Even football, where Hovis could crunch me if we were in the same game, was not as bad as cross-country running. Rimbold never jogged round with us, and out on the course I would be entirely alone. Sometimes Rimbold scanned the hillside with his binoculars to make sure we followed the correct line across the face of the slope. Other times he'd sit in his car at a point where we had to cross a lane between two fields, but more often than not he sat in his office with the kettle on and his feet up, doing a bit of this and that.

Today it looked like I was going to be on my own. If I bunked off, someone would be sure to see me, and if I hid, Rimbold would know that I hadn't been running because I wouldn't come back tired and covered in mud. I couldn't risk being caught and all that that would entail:

the phone call to Jeff's work and lunch-time detentions lacing and relacing Rimbold's old leather football, which he'd soak in muddy water until it was slimy and the laces went impossibly tight. He made kids work at that ball until their nails broke and their hands went numb. I'd rather take a chance on dodging Hovis out on the cross-country course than face Rimbold's wrath and more trouble at home.

Meanwhile Hovis had pushed off into a corner with his mates, and as I took my watch to the valuables-box they went ominously quiet and looked my way.

One or two keen kids jogged up and down on the spot to get warmed up. Then Rimbold locked up the valuables-box and called us together.

'Remember, no slacking. Full effort. Running all the way. No skiving off. No short cuts, and remember you're on show.' Those were fine words coming from the likes of him.

Rimbold set his watch and said, 'Now be off with you!'

We piled through the swing doors and raced down to the gate like a bunch of baboons on the apes' annual outing. Rimbold didn't even set a foot outside.

Hovis raced on ahead with Wilkes, while Jacko took up the rear. I thought I was going to crap myself, the way my stomach started to churn around. Although I felt like hugging the nearest drainpipe and screaming, I kept a grip on my feelings. If you run from a dog it chases you harder; I had to find some way of dodging around what-ever fate they had in store for me.

The cross-country course began on the estate next to the school. We had to run down Queens Road and turn first left into Bouncers Lane, past a scruffy selection of council houses. Bouncers Lane took us up to the foot of the hill, where a track began its run up the slope to an old wooden barn at the top. The barn was generally full of hay bales, and sometimes the farmer garaged his tractor there. It was a run-down affair with a leaking iron roof and was a favourite place for a smoke or a drink when kids bunked off.

The track up to the barn was bordered by a hedge and a ditch, and couldn't be seen from school. It wasn't until you turned left by the barn and ran across the hillside that you came into view of the school. Hovis would try to do me somewhere between the end of Bouncers Lane and the barn. The estate was too busy for him to attempt anything there.

I didn't like the idea of fat Jacko plodding on behind me, so I had to lose him, and then find some way of getting round behind the barn. The other kids were strung out in front of me all the way up Bouncers Lane, and I bobbed along, second to last, like an odd sock hung out to dry. I slowed to a breathless walk to gain some time. Jacko stopped and bent down, pretending to tie his shoelaces.

A few doors along the street a woman was coming out of her front gate, pushing two bawling children in front of her. I crossed the road so I'd pass her on the same side. I timed my walk to make sure that she'd pass Jacko, who was still fiddling with his laces, as I got to her front gate. When Jacko momentarily disappeared from sight behind the woman and her kids, I ducked down her garden path and round the back of the house.

The gardens were open at the back, scruffy and uncared for, divided from each other by single strands of wire running between concrete posts. With a little luck I could work my way across the gardens to the fields beyond, and make my way up to the barn on the other side of the hedge, out of sight. I just hoped Jacko was as stupid as I thought he was, and it would take him a little time to work out where I'd got to.

I went across five gardens without trouble, but as I was about to cross the sixth, the back door of the next house opened. I threw myself down behind a dustbin just in time, because as soon as I was out of sight a dog emerged on to the lawn. It circled the garden a couple of times with its nose to the ground; then cocked its leg against the clothes post. When it started to bark I thought the game was up. I was about to do a runner when I saw Jacko's fat form appear next door. His ugly mush was looking this way and that. The dog went for him. Then the door opened and there was a lot of commotion. Judging from the abusive language, Jacko was getting it in the neck. The door opened and shut again, and Jacko and the dog were gone.

I made it to the final garden with little difficulty after that, keeping close to the houses and ducking under the windows. Unfortunately, the last garden was hemmed in by a dense hedge where it adjoined the field. There was a radio playing in the house. Upstairs the curtains were drawn in the back bedroom. I could hear voices inter- mittently above the music coming from the radio. I crouched against the wall under the kitchen window, feeling miserably cold and exposed, desperately thinking what to do.

At the bottom of the garden was a shed nestling against the hedge.

I crept down the path and went round to the back of the shed, and squirmed my way into the gap between it and the hedge. I tried to climb up on to the roof, but there was nowhere to get a toehold. The more I wriggled, the more noise I made, and the thorny branches raked across my scrawny back. On the exposed side of the shed there was a water-butt made out of an old oil-drum, with a makeshift wooden lid. I had no choice but to try that way if I was to get up on to the shed roof and jump down into the field below.

I took hold of the downpipe and clambered up. The lid shifted ominously. Out of the corner of my eye I saw the bedroom curtain twitch. Then as I pushed with my foot to climb on to the roof, the wooden lid collapsed inwards with an almighty splash. I made a desperate lunge for the ridge of the roof and clung on. Once I'd scrambled to the top, I immediately lost my balance and fell head first into the top of the hedge. By now the door at the top of the garden had opened. A hairy man in a purple vest appeared, shouting:

'Oi, you! What the hell do you think you're at? Come here!'

There was no way I was going back up that path, having come this far. Scratched and bruised, my football shirt torn, I rolled off the hedge, and without looking back I hobbled off up the field as fast as I could go, thankful to be on the move again. I hugged the hedge and didn't stop until the shouting behind me had faded. I flopped down against a large hedgerow oak, well hidden from the houses.

Through the hedge I could just see the other runners in the distance strung out across the hillside. The afternoon settled into quiet. In the distance traffic hummed on the by-pass. There was no sign of Hovis and the rest.

My intention was to follow the hedge to the back of the barn and then continue on up the hill, veering away from the normal route. From the top of the hill I would descend at an angle across the slope and meet up with the proper path at the gate where the circuit crossed the lane, before dropping back down the hill to school beyond the allotments.

The first drops of rain then began to spatter down into the hedge. I prayed for the kind of downpour which would drive Hovis into the shelter of the barn.

I left the cover of the oak and cautiously approached the barn a few metres at a time, stopping occasionally to crouch down in the hedge to watch and listen. The weather worsened.

The barn loomed close in the driving rain, which now fell so heavily it drummed and steamed on the corrugated roof, and I could hear nothing inside the barn. Water cascaded from the gutter, preventing me from getting close enough to peer through the chinks in the planks into the dry warmth beyond.

The rain worked for me. I passed across the back of the barn without a sound. Soaked to the skin, but with considerable relief, I continued my dismal journey up the field.

I rested at the top in the dry shade of a tall beech, and as I peered round the huge trunk I saw Jacko and Wilkes leave the barn and cut a soggy path across the slope. Wilkes raced ahead, and Jacko lumbered along in his wake like a lame rhino, dropping further and further behind.

'Well, well, whatever have we here?'

It was Rimbold's voice. His sarcasm was unmistakable. I froze, with my back against the tree. There was nobody to be seen.

'It's the old football-lace treatment for you!' The voice came again from a slightly different angle, but subtly changed.

'Over here, gayboy.'

Then it dawned on me. Hovis appeared from behind a hawthorn bush to my right.

'Didn't know I was an impressionist, did you?'

I didn't say anything, but began to inch round the tree as he approached.

'Think you could give me the slip that easy? Jacko's a bit useless, but he'll get his too, soon enough. Met Mad Eddie creeping back from having a fag. Said he'd seen you rolling about on a hedge.'

There was no point running.

'Why don't you just leave me alone, Hovis?' I said.

'Why do you think?' he snarled, grabbing my shirt and pulling it tight under my chin. It formed a knot and he twisted it hard.

'Dunno,' I said, gasping for breath.

'You're more stupid than I thought then, if you don't know.'

Hovis let go of my shirt, twisted me round by the arm and kicked my legs away from underneath me. The next moment my face was being shoved into the dirt between the tree roots and Hovis was kneeling on my back with his trainers in my ears. He was doing something to my shoes. After what seemed like an eternity of agony he flipped me over on my back like I was a side of meat, and I saw that he'd tied my shoelaces together in impossible knots.

'That'll give you something to think about,' he said, standing up.

'Oh yeah, I forgot, I've got a present for yer.'

Then he kicked me hard in the ribs.

By the time I got my wind back he'd gone. I lay there aching all over and wondering what it was all about. What was I supposed to know, and why on earth did he keep picking on me? I was frozen, and soaked through.

I sat up miserably and looked at my laces. It was hopeless. I couldn't undo them if I tried. I tugged and twisted at my left shoe until it loosened enough to get it off. It was still attached to its companion, so I wound it round and round my right leg and secured it in place with my left sock. That way I could at least walk back to school. To protect my naked sole, I stripped off my football shirt and wound it round my foot, forming a makeshift shoe.

Looking like a cripple in search of a miracle, I hobbled back towards school.

Inevitably, I was late. Rimbold was waiting for me in the changing rooms, and so was the man in the purple vest. Hovis and his mates and all the rest sat silent on the benches, and that was the last I saw of them for a while, because I was pushed into the fetid air of Rimbold's office.

What followed, as you can imagine, was not pleasant. I had to apologize, Rimbold phoned my stepfather, and I was condemned to spend three lunch-times unlacing the 'sodding football' as Rimbold called it.

It was still only Tuesday.

Chapter 3

There was a mighty row when I got home from school. My mother was more silent than ever, but He went right up the wall. This was not at all unusual. 'He' was my stepfather, Jeff. I had to call him Jeff, unless I wanted to get clouted.

My father had left five years earlier, when I was ten, and Jeff had moved in a year ago. But Jeff had been around off and on for at least two years before that. Needless to say, we didn't get on. He was all right when he was just coming round to see my mum, but when he moved in, everything changed. There were new rules. What He said went. There was no arguing about it. My mother just clammed up and went along with it.

Rule Number One: we did what Jeff told us. Rule Number Two: I had to leave the house at six o'clock every evening and not come back until half past eight, when I was sent straight to bed. On Saturdays, I was allowed in the house afternoons only, and the same applied to Sundays.

So I used to get kicked out on to the streets, too early for Youth Club, which started at seven, while having to be back home early made it hardly worth the bother in the first place. Besides, Hovis went to the Club. Every day was the same: I tramped the streets around the estate and came back to bed to read comics by torchlight under the covers; I kept a big stock of *Marvel* comics under the bed.

Life was pretty difficult. Jeff wouldn't let me do

homework at home, because it would mean I'd have to stay in, so I had to get it all done at school, for what it was worth, and that wasn't much. It was just another potential source of trouble.

The only time I was allowed in the house before lock-up was when I had to babysit for my seven-year-old sister, Ginny. Sometimes I had to take her out too, not in the evenings, but on Saturdays or Sundays.

As I said, there was a mighty row in our house about the man in the purple vest. I could tell things were going to be bad before I got through the gate. It was only a quarter past four and Jeff's clapped-out Ford Granada was already parked on the hard-standing. I should have realized that Jeff was going to be trouble when he moved in. The first thing he did when he billeted himself in the house, which my mother had bought from the council, was to concrete over the flowerbeds at the front of the house, to create himself a parking space for his rusting heap.

Jeff had arrived home early, the front door was open, and I could hear him ranting and raving in the kitchen at the back of the house. I went down the side passage and listened for a while outside the kitchen window. My mother was trying to get a word in occasionally, without much success. They seemed to be arguing about two things. He was raging about my attitude, and my mum was on about something else, to do with money.

I couldn't avoid the situation for ever, so I pushed open the back door and went in. Ginny appeared in the door-way opposite, but my mum ushered her out without speaking to me and left me to face Him.

I tried to follow my mother into the hall, but Jeff got up and barred the way with his grubby arm. To me he was the Tatooed Stranger. A python, etched in green and pink, curled round the length of his arm, ending with its tongue stabbing at his wrist-watch. The python too was branded with the words, 'Hell Snakes of Steel'.

'Where do you think you're going?' he said.

'Upstairs,' I said, giving him the most defiant look I could muster.

'Like heck!' he said. 'I want to have words with you.'

He grabbed hold of my arm and shoved me down on to a chair, so my elbow banged hard against the table.

'The school's been on the phone to me at work. What have you got to say for yourself? Eh?' he shouted.

The blood vessels in his cheeks were broken under the surface of his skin. I suspected he drank too much. He was balding, past his peak, but still incredibly strong. His gut was big and bulged under his shirt, but not soft and flabby. I didn't answer him. I ignored him and flicked through the junk mail, which was piled up on the table.

'I'm talking to you,' he continued.

'You'll upset Ginny again,' I said, surprised at my coldness.

'Bugger Ginny! What I'm interested in, is what you've been getting up to when you're supposed to be out cross-country running. That's what I'm interested in!'

'I don't like running,' I hissed, and swept the pile of mail off the table.

He was about to clout me when my mother came back in.

'I'll make some tea,' she said.

'Not for him,' Jeff shouted, and my mum shrank back. 'He can go without.'

I didn't think he'd thump me while my mum was around, but he had other ways of getting to me.

My mum clattered about in the sink, filling the kettle and washing up the breakfast cups, while Jeff moved to perch on the edge of the table. The malevolent bastard towered above me. How my mum could bear him, I had no idea.

'Now listen!' he shouted, thumping his fist on the table. His signet ring raked into my knuckles. 'Now listen here, you! What were you doing in the garden?'

I wasn't going to tell him, and then get one of those 'stand up for yourself, fight like a man routines' I knew so well. That was all crap. A kid my size couldn't do anything about a kid like Hovis, or his mates. I'd got more sense than that.

'Leave him alone, please, Jeff,' my mother pleaded, feebly.

'You stay out of this! If you'd handled him properly in the first place, he wouldn't have turned out like this.'

He looked at her with total contempt. She kowtowed to him far too much.

'He's only a little lad,' she said but made no further gesture towards defending me. She would just turn her attention to some domestic chore or other and try to forget the whole thing.

'Go boil your head, Jeff!' I spat out his name, like I would a fly that had strayed into my mouth.

He was so taken by surprise that I had a chance to duck out of the kitchen and up the stairs. I fled into my room and pulled the chest of drawers across the door.

Surprisingly, Jeff didn't rush upstairs after me to kick the door down. The row rumbled on, without me, in the kitchen below. I could hear Ginny crying in the hall. I'd locked myself in my room, but Jeff knew he only had to play a waiting game.

So I flopped on to my bed and pulled the bedspread over me to keep warm. I was intent on sitting it out until six, when I hoped Jeff would want to get rid of me as usual. Ginny went to bed at six, and then Jeff demanded what he called 'peace and quiet' with my mother, and he couldn't get that when I was around, or so he said.

The only good thing about sharing the house with Jeff was that he got up and left in the morning while I was out doing my paper round, so that when I came back in for breakfast, he was usually gone.

Jeff was an HGV driver, and worked for a local removal firm. His area was confined to the South-West of England. If he'd been a long-distance, transcontinental trucker, away for weeks on end, I'd have been a lot happier, but as it was he came home most evenings, spending only the occasional night away.

He never took me with him in the holidays, and if he had we might have managed things better between us, but he wasn't that kind of bloke. He just cut me out, or kicked me around like an unwanted cat. I didn't really know anything about what he did or where he went. He left at half past seven and was back around six. Mostly I didn't see him much, except when there was trouble.

The arguments going on below subsided and the atmosphere in the house became subdued. The house itself was a drab and uninviting sort of place, but it was better to be there than walking the streets with no company except my gloomy thoughts.

At ten to six, I got out of bed and shifted the chest of drawers. My mother was coming out of the bathroom with Ginny, so I went out on to the landing.

'Kiss Wayne goodnight, there's a good girl,' she said. Ginny sidled up to me reluctantly, and I bent down and planted a kiss on her forehead.

'Goodnight, Ginny,' I said, and she trotted off into her room.

'I'll be there in a minute,' my mother called after her.

Downstairs the TV blared loudly in the lounge.

'Do try to be a bit politer to Jeff, Wayne. I've calmed him down for now. You'd better apologize when you see him next. I shouldn't go in now, though, before you go out.'

This seemed like sensible advice, so I said, 'Yeah, okay, if I must. I'll see you later.'

'I've made you some sandwiches.'

My mum looked small, and a lot older than she used to seem, worn down by all the trouble around her. Like an old handbag, she was shiny in the wrong places.

'Thanks,' I said, brushing past her. I went down the stairs, picked up the sandwiches and left by the back door. Jeff didn't stir from in front of the TV.

I'd spent a lot of nights like this in the last year, just wandering about in the streets. The beginnings of the dark evenings and the run up to Christmas had been the worst. In the late spring and early summer I could always pretend I was going somewhere or coming back from something important, but in winter I just felt self-conscious. Who in their right mind would be walking about in the freezing cold and wet? It was miserable, like going to the cinema on your own. In the light evenings at least I could hang around the rec with the little kids and play on the swings. If they had squabbles I'd act as peacemaker. If there was any bother amongst the junior kids they'd tell me about it, because 'Wayne can sort it out.'

When the dark nights came the little kids were kept in, and I only saw them on Saturdays and Sundays, and during the holidays.

The holidays weren't too bad, because Jeff wasn't around during the day, and my mum would let me stay in, except for the odd times when Jeff came home for lunch. Then I had to make myself scarce, and sometimes at very short notice.

The streets around our way were a network of concentric circles, connected with linking streets and walkways. The houses on the estate wore a uniform of ugly grey pebbledash, and stuck up like bad teeth behind unkempt privet hedges. The front doors were all painted the same unpleasant brown colour, except for the houses like mine, which had been bought from the council.

The streets were narrow and poorly lit. Stray dogs roamed about by day and night. Parked cars lined the streets on both sides and motorists were forced to zig-zag in and out. There was never anyone about on the winter nights, and I passed by unobserved.

Up the hill from us, on the other side of the railway line, the private housing began. The streets were wider and lighter, and more traffic passed along the roads. The houses sat comfortably beyond open-plan gardens. Silver birch and cherry trees lined the verges of the arterial road which ran through the estate. I didn't go up there much.

The town centre was three miles away, so I just wandered round and round our estate in ever-widening circles, and then back again. I was like a hamster on a treadmill.

Time passed slowly as I walked my usual beat. I was never one for inventing games in my head. My excursions were no more than cold, boring plods. I looked forward to getting back to bed and reading for half an hour under the covers with a torch.

Occasionally, I'd glance into the warm rooms of the houses I passed, and wish I was somebody else.

When I left the house after the row about the man in the purple vest, I was still angry, and I stormed off the estate abandoning my usual route. I walked fast and began to work up a sweat.

Eventually, I found myself at the pedestrian crossing, where the path traversed the railway line before leading up to the estate on the hill. I stopped and leant against the swing gate. The crossing was lit by a single spotlight, and the twin tracks disappeared into the darkness in both direction.

I went through the gate, but instead of crossing the line I turned left and walked along the tracks into the funnel of darkness. The lights of the houses on either side of the line seemed distant behind high garden fences.

The sound of trains flickering on the edge of our estate had always punctuated my evening walks, and helped to mark the passing of time. Five trains at half-hourly intervals would measure the time I was out.

I walked clumsily over the sleepers in the dark; my stride was either too short or too long. I stumbled onward, listening for the humming in the rails. The kids on the estate said you could never hear a train until it was too late, and once it had minced you up under its wheels no one would recognize you. Occasionally, there'd been cases in the paper where people, usually old ladies, had put their necks on the line. There had been deaths on the crossing in the past.

One story that was frequently told in the rec was about a headless workman patrolling the line at night in a luminous orange jacket, while another involved a naked lady, but they were just stories put about to keep the kids away from the railway. No one came near here at night.

The kids on the estate said that if you were hit by a train you wouldn't feel a thing. I kept walking. My anger began to recede, and the cold took hold. I began to skip on and off the rails to keep warm as I bumbled along, and at about the tenth skip, as my foot touched the rail, the line began to hum.

My head seemed to turn inside out and my eardrums clattered like cymbals blown about by a maelstrom inside a steel box. My knees jerked up through my shoulders. My heart stopped. Then it started pumping again, so fast it started to roar.

Someone was screaming. It was me. Then there was the sound of falling chippings and my body rolling down the embankment. I crashed into the fence and lay on my back. Still. The drumming in my head faded.

What I saw then, glowing in the dark, was a glasshouse. If you've seen brightly lit carriage windows flicker nervously across the night like the frames of an old movie, then you'll know what I mean when I say the glasshouse had the opposite effect. Before me, on the other side of the fence, it appeared as a capsule of light floating serenely a fraction above the surface of the ground. Its stillness after my tumble down the embankment was a comfort. I stared at it from where I lay nursing my bruises, until its light suddenly snapped out.

I listened intently. An owl hooted distantly and traffic droned down the main road. The glasshouse door slid open with a metallic rasp, and heavy boots crunched along a gravel path. There was a faint cough, a door banged and a motorcycle started to move off. Aromatic tobacco smoke drifted across the night in a delicate cloud.

Above me a goods train rattled past and rumbled off into the distance. In the silence that followed I ducked under the wire fence and crept towards the glasshouse, but before I reached the dark structure there came the sound of the motorcycle returning. I hobbled back to the fence and scrambled back up the embankment. Picking myself up at the top, I stumbled off towards home, but I already had it in my mind to return when I felt better.

Chapter 4

Next day I got into school as the bell went and kids were disappearing into the building in dribs and drabs. It was Assembly day, so I made my way down the dark and gloomy main corridor and dumped my bag and coat outside the hall. No one was very keen to go in, but when the tutors finally arrived we were herded inside.

Assembly always began chaotically and was usually half over before everybody settled down. Crease wandered round at the front, pretending he was busy, until there was no alternative but to shuffle his papers on the lectern and make repeated requests for quiet. His cheery 'Good morning, Stirling House!' was greeted with groans and mutters.

Then the Headmaster, a tall, tanned, but ungainly man, shambled up to the lectern. He treated us to a rambling account about his next-door neighbour's pig and his wife's string of pearls. We'd all heard it before when we were in the second year, but its meaning was still no clearer; perhaps because no one listened. Assembly was a time for dozing or passing notes up and down the rows of chairs. Appointments were made through garbled games of Chinese Whispers. Assembly was only a little more ordered than registration. No one really knew what it was for.

By the time I got out of Assembly, my bag and coat were gone. If I didn't find them Jeff would kill me; the week was turning out to be a particularly bad one. I hung around outside the hall until everyone had gone, but neither coat nor bag was anywhere to be seen. Crease and the tutors had left the hall when the Head started to drone on at us, and there was no one around to report it to. I couldn't be late for French, so I had to forget about it until break.

It was hopeless without my bag. I'd have to borrow a pen, and that always caused trouble, because nobody would lend me one at first and then Sharla would reluctantly come to my rescue. Then I'd have to do all my work on paper and copy it up afterwards, if I found my books, and if not, I'd have to buy new books and copy up a whole term's work. There would be no time to do it in school, and I wouldn't be allowed to at home. The whole thing looked very bad.

Even though I hurried, I was still late to French and everyone was already sat down. Mr Johnson was at the front, trying to get everyone quiet, and demanding homework in at the same time. He was weird. He was a big bloke, thickset and vaguely unshaven. Johnson was approaching forty, but he always wore pale blue jeans and a black leather jacket. His teardrop chromatic glasses made him look like an American motorcycle cop. Johnson was really juvenile. He had posters of gay pop stars all over his wall. He liked the kind of music twelve-year-olds like, and he insisted on playing it during his lessons, while we got on with our work. Johnson was still going through puberty. Puberty's a difficult time, Sharla would say.

'Ah, bonjour, Twiggy. Comment allez-vous?' he said as I came through the door. Nobody, but nobody, spoke French in Johnson's lessons, so I didn't reply. I plonked myself down next to Sharla and Becca, who'd saved a place for me.

'Be like that then!' snapped Johnson, his voice rising and falling as though it was about to break. The class groaned.

Sharla bent her wrist and blew him a kiss, but Johnson didn't notice.

The noise in the room rose.

'Homework! I've got one ... two ... three ... eight books here,' he shouted. 'There's twenty of you. Now where are they?'

He looked at me.

'Twigs, where's yours?'

'Someone's nicked my bag,' I said, looking sheepish.

'You mean, you haven't done it.'

Then Sharla shouted out, 'He has, sir, I saw him do it in the library on Monday.'

Johnson shut up then and turned on the others. He was a bit unstable. The lesson wasn't going to be easy.

Johnson started to bellow in frustration, going red in the face like a blood orange.

'Get your books out and put them on the table in front of you.'

Then he ordered us to put our hands on our heads, like prisoners of war. No one seemed very keen to take him on.

We were seeing the wrong side of Johnson. Sometimes, though, he was dead pally and put his arms round the lads, and let us call him by his first name, Wally, which was a bit unfortunate. Then he'd play our music tapes over the Language Lab equipment and we'd pretend to work while he impersonated well-known disc jockeys, and these Radio Wally sessions were a good laugh. Other times he'd tell us how he hated French people, but that the food, wine and the sunshine were what he liked about France. Johnson was off his rocker, and parents were always complaining about him, but nothing was ever done. He was Head of Faculty and he was a law unto himself. Needless to say no one passed French in his class.

So we sat there with our hands on our heads, not daring

to breathe as he walked up and down the rows examining our books. When he got to Sharla, he saw that she hadn't got her book. Johnson put both hands on the table, so his knuckles stood out white. He leaned menacingly towards us. His eyes reminded me of pickled onions in a jar, and his breath smelt of garlic and stale cigars.

'Gor, what have you been eating, sir?' screeched Becca, so suddenly overcome by revulsion that she forgot herself.

'What?' he exploded. 'What did you say?'

The spell was broken and everyone erupted, some laughing, others jabbering and gibbering in amazement.

Johnson spat and spluttered, pulled our table away from in front of us, and hurled it over on to the floor, scattering the kids in the next row, who leapt from their seats and ducked for cover.

'Leave her alone!' I shouted, and stood up between the raving lunatic and Becca.

'Sit down!' he yelled, grabbing my shoulder.

'No,' I said defiantly, falling back on to the floor amongst a heap of books and furniture. Becca, meanwhile, had the presence of mind to flee from the room.

Johnson left me in a heap, and proceeded to tear up all our exercise books one by one and jump on them like a little kid having a temper tantrum. There was a stunned silence which lasted until he stormed out of the room.

The room gradually returned to normal as we realized that what we had witnessed was what had happened many times before. Johnson had simply exploded. Johnson was off his rocker and, ultimately, nobody in our school cared.

Nothing would happen to us, or Becca for being rude, because tomorrow Wally would be fine again and playing music. He didn't want his routine disturbed.

A long time ago we had cottoned on to the fact that it wasn't worth complaining, because the teacher was always right, and everybody knew how temperamental Mr Johnson was, so it was our own fault if we provoked him. The whole thing would blow over.

Johnson didn't seem to be in a hurry to return to the lesson, so Sharla and I wandered off in search of Becca. We found her in the girls' toilets, off the main corridor.

For some reason Sharla dragged me in too and slammed the door. I protested, but she told me that if I wanted to nick off lessons, then I might as well learn to do it properly. Becca was busying herself at the mirror as if nothing had happened. She'd had run-ins with Johnson before, and she knew when it was time to make herself scarce.

When she realized I was there, Becca said, 'Thanks, Wayne, for sticking up for me. I didn't know you had it in you.'

'Neither did I!' I said, feeling myself turning a beetroot colour. 'Never thought I'd end up in the girls' toilets either.'

'Yeah, well, just keep your voice down, that's all.'

We had about thirty minutes to kill before the next lesson, so I sat down on the floor. My body ached all over from my fall the night before. Sharla and Becca ignored me, preferring to mess about with hairspray in front of the mirror.

They gossiped about all the usual things: who was going out with who, and who wasn't any more. But then they started on about a train stopping short of the station, at the bottom of Sharla's garden, and the police coming out to look along the line. Sharla's neighbours were sure someone had been killed, and there was a rumour going round that a body was found by sniffer dogs, and that the head was still missing. This made me feel sick. I staggered into a cubicle and puked up in the pan.

'You all right, Wayne?' Sharla said. She didn't have time

to say more, because there was a movement outside the toilets, and they both scuttled into the cubicle after me and bolted the door. Becca pulled the chain and I got my head out of the way just in time before I got drenched.

'Keep quiet,' Sharla whispered. 'Try not to be sick again, or we'll be for it.'

I hung on to the toilet bowl, while Sharla and Becca wedged themselves either side of me. I closed my eyes and held my breath.

The door of the bogs opened and closed. I couldn't tell whether anyone had come in or not, and from the reaction of the girls I knew that they didn't know either. We waited.

It was news to me that the train, which had so nearly killed me, had come to a halt further up the line, and that the police had been out looking for me. I had jumped instinctively as the train came upon me from behind, unseen. I had rolled down the embankment as the train went thundering past.

I was a little bruised and shaken, but none the worse for wear, and had walked back to the estate when I'd recovered my senses.

Jeff's car was gone when I got back to the house, so I risked going in. Because I looked so pale, my mother didn't need much persuading to let me in early.

We were just beginning to get fidgety in the confined space of the toilet cubicle when a voice said, 'Right, you've had long enough. OUT!'

It was Hovis.

No one moved. Hovis banged on the door, and whispered in a simpering voice, 'Come on, who's in there?'

At this point Becca spoke up.

'Me and Sharla,' she said. 'We thought you were Johnson.'

'What? That gay git, you've got to be joking!'

The girls opened the door. Sharla emerged first and took Hovis by the arm and led him towards the door. Becca shoved me behind the toilet door and said softly so Hovis couldn't hear, 'Shut up or else.'

She knew about me and Hovis.

'What are you doing down here?' Becca asked as she went up to him.

'What do you think?' he said. 'Boys' toilets aren't safe any more, haven't you heard?'

'And whose fault is that?' snapped Sharla in that sarcastic way she saves for people she doesn't like.

'Bog off!' Hovis shouted. Then he did something to Sharla, because she screamed and lashed out at him.

'Bitch!' screamed Hovis.

'Serves you bloody right!' said Becca to Hovis.

Then the door slammed shut. The girls were gone. Hovis began to pace up and down. I was jammed behind the door in the end cubicle. I hoped Hovis wouldn't look that far.

Fortunately, Hovis went into the cubicle nearest the door. Then there were a lot of rustling sounds followed by a very soggy splash. Hovis grunted with pleasure and pulled the chain. After that I couldn't hear what was going on, because the plumbing made such a row as the cistern filled up.

When the pipes eventually stopped hissing and rattling there was silence in the toilets. Hovis was gone.

Right in front of me, as I came out of the cubicle, scrawled on the wall in large red letters was the message:

'GAYBOY YOUR DEAD'

I ran out of the toilets, and straight into Crease. My head thumped into his beer belly and he emitted an audible 'whoosh' as he staggered backwards.

'Eh! Hang on . . . Hang on! What's the hurry, Wayne?' he said, gasping for breath.

I mumbled something about the boys' toilets being locked, and being too desperate to go over to New Block. The first part was true. The boys' bogs were locked as from today, because of trouble and damage. Someone had put cling-film over the pans again.

Crease could have let the matter drop then and there, but he obviously didn't have enough to do that morning, or else he was looking for an excuse to go creeping into the girls' toilets.

'Let's have a look and see what you've been up to. I wasn't too impressed by what Mr Rimbold told me yesterday.'

He took hold of the back of my neck and frog-marched me back in. There was the writing on the wall, and what was worse, there was all my work stuffed down the toilet. My red felt-tipped pen was on the floor by the toilet bowl and my carrier bag was dangling from the cistern.

Things looked pretty bad, and that's how I got myself suspended.

I couldn't tell Crease about Hovis, without getting Sharla and Becca into trouble for running out of French. The evidence was damning, and others before me had tried to blame Hovis for things they'd done. Besides, I knew very well that Hovis hadn't been in Assembly, because he was off nicking my coat and bag, and hadn't been registered. Crease would see clearly from the records that he wasn't in school, and when Wally Johnson told everyone in the staffroom that I'd been rude to him, and how he'd put me in my place, it would be obvious that I'd have a grudge against him. As it was common knowledge that all the kids thought Wally Johnson was gay, you didn't have to be a genius to work out that the 'gayboy' of the message written with my red pen referred to him.

Later, Hovis entered the school office at ten-thirty and signed the Late Book, and that put the cap on it. Then he had the gall to present Crease with a faked-up dental appointment card, and Crease swallowed it, which was a bit rich, because even I knew Hovis had been fitted with false teeth after his last few good ones had been knocked out by his father the previous year.

Meanwhile, Johnson had returned to class a few minutes after we'd left; he got to Becca and Sharla, and threatened them with making their lives a misery if they said anything about the row in the lesson. They told Johnson I was being sick in the toilets and would be out for the rest of the lesson. Then everything returned to normal. He even gave out new exercise books and started broadcasting Radio Wally again.

The only good thing to come out of all this was that I wouldn't have to suffer Rimbold's football-lace torture at lunch-time, nor for the rest of the week. And more important, I would get some relief from Hovis.

As I sat outside Crease's office at break, waiting for him to have the letter to my mother typed, Sharla and Becca turned up. They'd heard a rumour that I was in trouble, and were feeling a little guilty about abandoning me in the bogs, although they'd thought that was the best thing to do at the time. They were much friendlier towards me than usual and seemed to be taking a genuine interest.

The corridor outside Crease's office was crowded with kids hanging about. Crease wasn't there and no one was on duty. Thick cigar smoke was drifting in blue clouds from Mustapha's office next door. The door was slightly ajar and the smoke began to form a ground mist along the length of the corridor.

Sharla pulled up another chair, and Becca sat down on the floor beside her and gazed after the fifth-year boys as they passed.

'What's going on?' Sharla asked.

She really was quite pretty in a cosy sort of way. Becca rummaged through her bag for her lipstick.

'I've been suspended,' I said matter-of-factly.

'What?' Becca shouted, closing her handbag with a snap. 'You're joking!'

'It's true,' I said. 'Crease caught me coming out of the bogs. I'm getting done for writing on the wall and trying to flush my books down the pan.'

'You didn't, did you?' said Sharla, as though she half believed that I was capable of doing that sort of thing!

'Course not,' I said. 'It was Hovis, when you left, but I can't tell Crease that can I?'

'Why not? I would,' said Becca indignantly, and got up off the floor, intent on seeing Mustapha about it.

'No, don't,' I said, grabbing hold of her and pulling her back. 'You'll just get into trouble for being in the bogs as well, and you'll get done for the writing too. Anyway, Hovis can prove he wasn't in school at the time. Besides, I don't mind. After the row I had last night, this can't make much difference. Three days away from this dump suits me fine. I'm really peed off with it.'

Sharla looked interested. She liked a bit of juicy domestic gossip, but she spoke to me in a concerned sort of way, which suggested there was more to her interest than that.

'What row?' she said.

Becca sat down again and tuned in. She did everything Sharla did.

'Oh, you know, I had a big bust up with my stepdad over this thing about the cross-country.'

I filled them in on all the details, but I was careful to leave out the bit about my scrape with the train. Then the bell went before they could inquire further, and they had to go off to their next lesson.

'See you on Monday. Have a nice time!' Sharla said with a smile as she went.

'Thanks,' I said. 'Can you keep your eye out for my coat? I'll get done if I can't find it.'

I thought it would be nice if I could see Sharla before Monday, but she lived on Hovis territory. Anyway, she didn't really like me. She just put up with me at school, because she felt sorry for me.

Crease came back shortly after the bell and took me into his office. Then Mustapha Crap came in, bringing all his foulness with him.

They made me sit in a chair while they explained what was going to happen to me, and then they got all sympathetic and asked me about my problems, and started poking their noses into my family business. They wanted to know why I was going 'off the rails' (that was a laugh!) and 'exhibiting deviant tendencies', whatever that meant.

I didn't say anything, and that seemed to fox them. They met a wall of silence, and that made them mad. Mustapha then threatened me with County Hall or something if I didn't grow up and pull myself together. He said he was a busy man and couldn't waste time on the likes of me.

Crease was a smarmy git and Mustapha was just pathetic.

Chapter 5

My mum was out when I got home later that morning. The house was locked up, and I didn't have a key, so I went round the side of the house to the shed at the bottom of the garden. It was padlocked as usual. Without my coat, I was freezing. Getting into the shed was my only hope of keeping warm until my mum got home. It was still only twelve-thirty.

I searched in my pencil case for my 15 cm steel ruler. At least Hovis had left me that. The ruler was just thin enough to be a fairly effective screwdriver. I got to work on the shed door straight away. The screws came away from the latch without much difficulty, and soon the padlock was dangling loose and I was free to get inside.

It was a lot warmer inside the shed, out of the wind. Hanging up from the door was one of Jeff's old jackets, so I put it on to keep warm until I got the Camping Gaz stove working.

Finding the matches proved a little more difficult. I checked the jacket pockets and pulled out every drawer of the work-bench. There were no matches to be found, but I did come across a cigarette lighter. When I flicked the wheel it proved to be useless. There was no fuel left, and I could only get a thin spark, not enough to light the gas. I succeeded in making the shed smell, that was all.

Jeff had put up the small work-bench at the end of the shed, and I sat down on the old swivel chair he'd brought back from work, and played around with the odds and ends arrayed on the work-surface.

I'd just about given up on the idea of getting any heat when I noticed a single match lying on the floor. It was wedged under a gallon can of motor oil, the red tip just protruding. Jeff had obviously dropped it one time he came in for a quiet fag while I got on with the washing up.

Fortunately the match was still live and dry. I struck it on a rusty file, and lit the stove.

The shed was about eight feet long and four feet wide, with a window to one side which looked out on to the garden. It was full of old cans stacked on shelves and bits and pieces to do with the car: old handbrake cables, ramps, antifreeze, brake fluid, a rusty fog-lamp; all the usual stuff. Jeff's bike leaned against the wall opposite the window. He never used it now he was letting himself go to fat, and he never let me use it either.

I made a mental catalogue of all this junk, not because any of it would be of any use to me, but just to pass the time. I wasn't allowed in the shed, and the place aroused my curiosity.

After a while the sun burst through a hole in the gloomy February sky and momentarily cast a light across the floor of the shed, before disappearing again. In the place where the oil can had been standing before I moved it to get at the match I saw that one of the planks was slightly raised at one end. When I looked more closely I could see that it had been cut. The cut showed as a straw-coloured line. It had been fairly recently made.

I took a closer look. The plank was firmly nailed in place. The nails were newer than the others. They'd only recently begun to rust. For some reason Jeff had taken out a section of one plank and then put it back again. It didn't make much sense to me. It was the sort of thing a small boy with a secret stash of sweets might do, but not a grown man. There was no new electrical wiring in evidence, and certainly no plumbing, so it couldn't be anything to do with that.

I would have liked to have had a look underneath, but time was not on my side and I didn't know how to do it without leaving any incriminating evidence of interference behind.

I decided to leave it until later. I put out the stove and hung the jacket back up on the rusty nail behind the door.

Getting the bracket which held the padlock back on to the shed door was a lot more difficult than removing it. The screws seemed a little slack, or else the holes in the wood were too large, and it was not easy to realign it exactly with the pale impression it had left on the creosoted wood.

When I'd accomplished the job to my satisfaction and rubbed a little dirt around the edges of the bracket, I sat down on the doorstep to wait for my mother to come home.

Thinking about the mystery of the shed floor kept my mind off Crease's letter, which was burning a hole in my trouser pocket.

'And where's your coat? Did you flush that down the toilet too, or did you just throw it away?'

My mother was livid, and I was going to get one of those 'money doesn't grow on trees' lectures. I'd been through this before.

'Look, I told you, Mum, I don't know where my coat is. I didn't have time to look for it before they sent me home. Someone's probably moved it for a joke or taken it by mistake. It'll turn up.'

I don't think I sounded too hopeful, and my explanation certainly didn't do anything to placate my mother.

'That coat cost at least £25.00. It didn't come from the market, you know. Where are you going to get that kind of money from, eh?'

I was already handing over most of my paper-round money to help towards my keep.

'Well, I'll just have to give you all my paper-round money until it's paid off. Won't I?'

'And how long is that going to take, and where's the money coming from in the meantime? Tell me that! Money doesn't grow on trees you know. I don't work, and Jeff doesn't give me much. As it was, I had to get round him to buy you that coat. It'll be summer before I can afford another. You know he has the Family Allowance off me every month for the mortgage.'

We were sat at the kitchen table and getting nowhere.

'And as for this other business, I don't know what Jeff will say when he finds out. I don't know how I'll tell him.'

My mother looked at the ceiling in despair and wrung her handkerchief between her hands.

'Why do you have to tell him?' I said. 'The letter's addressed to you, not him. He's nothing to do with me anyway.'

My mum obviously hadn't thought about this possibility, she was so used to living under Jeff's thumb. She stopped wringing her hands for a moment and a tiny gleam appeared in her eye.

'But what if the neighbours see you, Wayne, or hear something? You're not the only kid from that school around here you know. What if they say something to Jeff?'

'Oh, well, tell him if you like. I'm sure he'll really want to take the morning off work to come up to school on Monday to get me readmitted,' I added sarcastically.

'Don't be like that!' she snapped, looking hurt. 'Go on, get to your room before he comes back!'

I knew that she wouldn't say anything. The letter would be torn up and put in the boiler before Jeff got home. She didn't want trouble from Jeff any more than I did.

Jeff was in a good mood at tea. He'd had a win on the horses. My mum had a go at him about risking his money, but when he laid out two hundred quid in fivers on the table next to the toaster that changed things. He sat there and smiled like the original Burger King, what with his pint of lager to his right, *Evening Post* to the left, and minute steak and chips in the middle. He was so chuffed with himself, he didn't have time to bother with me.

He held the paper in one hand and shovelled in food with the other. Every now and then the paper would rustle as he wiped his chin with the back of his hand. I'd seen kids at school eat better.

While he lorded it in the kitchen, my mother to-and-froed between the table and cooker, adding to the meal and clearing up as she went along.

Jeff studied the sports pages while I tried to read the front as it dipped in and out of its own shadow.

There was a small headline at the bottom of the front page: 'MYSTERY SIGHTING ON LINE'. I read on as best I could, trying not to show any interest at all.

It mentioned the train stopping short of the station, and the subsequent search with tracker dogs, and most incriminating of all, the story clearly stated that the only clue to be found was a packet of cheese and pickle sandwiches, freshly made. The driver was convinced he saw something, but the search had revealed nothing. Then it said 'Continued on Page 2.' Jeff usually took the paper off to the bog or down to the shed after tea, so there wasn't much chance of finding out any more. It would be used to light the boiler before I could get a look at it.

All this was swimming around my mind when Jeff interrupted my thoughts.

'Here,' he said, 'have a fiver.'

I looked at him in disbelief.

'Come on, take it before I change my mind.'

He was stripped down to his string vest and his tattoo stirred menacingly. I wasn't about to argue, so I took the money.

'Thanks,' I said, 'but what's it for?'

'Bad luck not to share in luck,' he said mysteriously, and went back smugly to his paper.

Jeff occasionally had these moments of generosity. I would pay him back by turning the fiver over to my mother.

At six o'clock, despite Jeff's benevolent mood, I was chucked out as usual. Because I had no coat, I was wearing two shirts and two pullovers and a pair of my mum's old mittens. They were too small, but better than nothing. Fortunately, it was dark, so no one would see the pandas embroidered on them.

As soon as I was out of the house I made straight for the railway line again. I turned left at the crossing and this time walked beside the tracks rather than between them. By the time the first train hurtled past I was already flattened against the embankment. When it had gone I stood up and stared down at the glasshouse which blazed before me like a spaceship in the night.

For all those years that I had lived on the estate and walked up the main road to school I had not known of its existence. It could have just landed there, for all I knew, after a long journey across space; a ship masquerading as a huge greenhouse. It was no such thing; but it looked just as alien, glowing brightly amongst all the industrial clutter which had accumulated round our area.

It stood alone on a plot of land behind the scrap-metal merchant's, which fronted on to the main road, the way I took to school. The glasshouse was in a slight hollow and hidden from view behind the piles of old cars which filled the scrapyard.

From where I stood, on the other side of the fence, the glasshouse looked enormous, and its light cast the world beyond its realm into impenetrable darkness. Its halo of light fell short of where I leaned against the fence.

I could see an old man shuffling about inside with an old fertilizer sack. He was smoking a pipe. He disappeared behind a screen of tall plants when he came to the far end of the glasshouse, and then the lights went out.

When I was sure he had gone, I ducked under the fence like I had on the previous occasion. Crouching down behind a large water-butt at the rear of the glasshouse, I waited. There was the familiar hoot of an owl, the traffic droned along the main road, but there was no indication that the motorbike was about to return. I skirted all the way round the glasshouse, stopping to listen at each corner. I could see quite well when my eyes adjusted. The building purred, its fans clicking on and off, breaking the silence of the quiet garden, for a garden it appeared to be. The glasshouse seemed to breathe in the dark. A high brick wall enclosed the garden on three sides. At the far end of the garden stood a house. Its silhouette rose in the gloom. It was quiet and without a single light showing.

I couldn't tell whether the land in between was

cultivated, left to grow wild or laid to lawn. A path stretched away from the glasshouse. The door was held fast with a padlock.

Then I lost my nerve and crept back to the fence to decide what to do. The dark and shadowy garden seemed a remote and forbidding place, but the glasshouse itself offered hope of warmth on a cold February night. If only I could get inside, neither Jeff nor Hovis nor anybody else would be able to find me there. The glasshouse offered an end to my lonely evening walks.

It had become increasingly obvious that there was no one in the house, and it was unlikely that I would be disturbed. Once I'd conquered my fear of the dark, I plucked up courage to take another look.

I felt my way slowly along each side, peering up and down. The wooden framework of the glasshouse was mounted on a low brick wall about three feet high. The woodwork and brickwork were sound. There wasn't a single pane of glass out of place. The building had been lovingly maintained. There was no obvious way in.

There were ventilating lights in the roof, which opened upwards, but these were shut. Anyway it was beyond my capabilities to scale the vertical framework, spider across the roof and then make the long drop to the floor below.

The more I saw of the glasshouse, and the more hopeless breaking in seemed to be, the more I wanted to get inside. It was a challenge, and because there'd be no other kids around to laugh at my fumbling efforts, because it could be my secret task, I felt I might, in the end, be able to rise to the occasion. I began to recognize a sense of resolve within myself which I had never called on. The glasshouse seemed to be out of this world, and I was fired by the thought of what secrets were waiting to be discovered within.

50

The door revealed nothing. There was no name board declaring what the place was. It looked too big to be a private greenhouse, or at least it was not like any I'd seen before. It must have cost a fortune to build, and another fortune to keep going.

There were no credit-card stickers on the windows and no sign inside of advertisements like the ones at the garden centre near school. So there were no clues from that angle.

The padlock was heavy and unyielding, more secure than the lock of Jeff's garden shed.

The whole thing needed a little thought, but it was too cold to hang about for long. I seemed to have a lot to think about. I had more on my mind than I'd had for a long time, but there was nothing more I could do right now, so I climbed back up the embankment and made my way slowly homeward.

When I came in through the back door and switched on the light, the first thing I noticed was my coat hanging over the chair next to the boiler. It had obviously been soaking wet.

Jeff had heard me come in, and appeared in the doorway.

'Some friends of yours came round.'

From the way he said it, I knew he was no longer in a benevolent mood.

'I didn't know I had any,' I said.

'Don't get funny with me.' He was barring the way out of the kitchen.

'I'm not, I mean it,' I said. 'Who's been round?'

'Two girls.'

'Oh?'

'What's been going on then? Why did you leave your coat at school?'

I didn't know what my mother had told him, so I tried to hedge.

'I don't know,' I said. Sometimes even I thought I sounded feeble, and this was one of those occasions.

'What do you mean, you don't know?' he screamed.

I said nothing and looked at the floor.

'Answer me!' he shouted, starting forward and grabbing my wrist. 'Look at me when I'm talking to you, you rude little git.'

'You're hurting me,' I said, trying to pull my hand away, but he twisted it harder, giving me a searing Chinese burn.

'Out with it, or I'll knock your block off!'

'I thought I'd lost it. I looked, but I couldn't find it,' I winced.

He twisted my arm round behind my back and grabbed me by the throat, forcing my chin up with his forearm. I began to cry. Then my mother came in.

'Get off him!' she screamed.

She clawed at Jeff wildly, but he pushed her off with his foot and sent her sprawling into the kitchen table, where she lost her balance and crashed on to the floor.

While Jeff was distracted by this, I writhed about and got my right heel off the ground, high and hard enough to dead-leg him in the thigh. He lost his grip on my arm and let me go.

Jeff was between me and the back door, so I escaped into the hall and fumbled at the front door. The security chain was on and the door was bolted. Before I could get it undone, Jeff was hobbling into the hall. He was still able to move fast, like a rhino with a rupture, and mad for blood.

I turned on my heel and dashed up the stairs before he could pounce on me. I crashed through my bedroom door with Jeff close behind screaming all kinds of obscenities. There was no time to bar the door. I scrambled across the bed and grappled with the window catch. It wouldn't budge, so I gave it all I'd got. I was propelled by fear. The window burst open as Jeff made a lunge for my leg. His fist crashed into the sill as I leapt.

The darkness whistled past me. I didn't fly. I didn't perform any death-defying stunts. I simply fell with a sickening crunch, and my brain whirled around my skull like liver in a liquidizer.

Fear and panic drove me to my feet and despite the pain in my knee I hobbled round the side of the house and tumbled into Sharla and Becca as they came down the path.

'Wayne, are you all right?' Sharla said.

'Yeah, fine,' I said, and collapsed in a heap against the old Granada. My knee had finally packed up.

Before they could say anything more, Jeff came out of the front door. By the time he reached us, he was as nice as pie.

'Are you all right, son? What happened?' he asked, like any normal father would. He was bending over me like a football trainer with his magic sponge. Sharla stared at me in total bewilderment, not quite sure what to say. Becca was equally confused, and waiting for a lead from her friend.

'I've twisted my knee,' I said. 'I don't think I can get up.'

By now my mum had come out as well but, seeing that my friends were there, she said nothing.

Sharla helped Jeff get me on to my feet, and I hobbled to the house between them. On the doorstep my mum thanked Sharla and Becca for their help, and then thanked them again for returning my coat, before ushering them quickly down the garden path without further explanation. I was dumped on the sofa in the lounge, and didn't have a chance to say goodbye to them. If they hadn't turned up to check that I was all right I don't know what would have happened.

After they'd gone, things quietened down. Jeff was sullen, but calmer, and in a short while he disappeared off to the pub. I got the rare opportunity of watching TV.

My mother explained that when the girls brought my coat round, they let slip about me being suspended. It didn't happen as baldly as that. They told Jeff they thought they'd better bring the coat round, because they wouldn't be seeing me until the following week. Then Jeff had started asking questions and the secret was out.

One good thing came out of all this, and that was that I got to stay in bed all day Thursday, because when I woke up in the morning, my leg hurt like crazy.

My mother brought me breakfast in bed when she came back from doing my paper round, and it was my turn to feel like a king. Jeff had gone out without looking in or saying goodbye, and I had breathed a sigh of relief when I heard the car start.

I had the whole day ahead of me, and I felt what most kids feel on the first day of a holiday. I'd not felt like that for a very long time.

I drifted in and out of sleep, and entered that realm of warm semi-wakefulness where anything is possible and dream pictures are there to be manipulated. As I turned my head to the wall, plumped up the pillows and submerged beneath the blankets, I kept the real world at bay, and felt I had the power to do anything.

The glasshouse rose out of the earth before me and towered over my head. It flashed on and off like a great beacon. I stood before it, arms outstretched. I saw myself as a bold silhouette on a science-fiction movie hoarding.

54

The glasshouse changed colour and pulsed. I was drawn inside and found myself in an enormous chromium hall. I observed it coolly through my expensive German sunglasses. A huge silver screen floated in the air at one end of the hall, and on it was a vast image of a torrent of white water plummeting down a black rockface. As the water hit the bottom edge of the screen, it gushed over into a wide pool which covered the far end of the chromium hall.

A voice boomed out of the atmosphere.

'Welcome home, Hawkmaster, Lord of the Skies, King of all that lies beyond the Mountains of Mars, Champion of the Meek, and Slayer of the Hell Snakes of Steel . . .'

The voice was about to say more, but my mother appeared with a cup of coffee and took the breakfast tray away. I often had fanciful waking dreams like that where I played a role far different from the one I was stuck with in reality. The trouble was, they never lasted very long and in the cold light of day they just seemed stupid.

I dozed off and on throughout the morning, but was never able to summon up again the image of the chromium hall, the Hawkmaster and the voice within. But I could see the glasshouse clearly, as I remembered it burning intensely in the night like a vast beacon, beckoning me to return. I told myself I would go back there at the first opportunity, boldly and in broad daylight.

When I finally got up in the late afternoon, I limped across to the mirror to take a look at myself. There had been no miraculous transformation. I was no Lord of the Skies, or anything like any of the super-heroes I had read about in the comics I kept under the bed for my torchlight reading sessions; I was just spotty old Wayne looking pathetic, like a hospital patient, in my striped pyjamas. There was no magic in what I saw. All I could feel was the pain in my knee and a draught coming through the crutch of my pyjama trousers.

I took my pyjama jacket off and flexed my muscles in front of the mirror. I was pimply and pasty. I had a long way to go before I began to look normal, let alone become a muscle rippling super-hero.

The mirror was only two feet square and mounted half-way up the wall, so I climbed on the bed to take a look at my legs. With my pyjama bottoms off, completely naked, I looked even worse, like something a vulture had picked the meat off and left on the side of its plate. I looked like a blind creature from the deep, all pale and slimy.

I climbed back into bed feeling very disappointed, and glumly took stock of my situation. I was pathetic, and something had to be done.

All of a sudden I had a barmy idea, and shot out of bed again. I slipped into my jeans and rifled my drawers to find my rugby shirt. Then I went to the bathroom and grabbed a towel.

What I did next still surprises me, but it made me feel better at the time. I rolled up the towel and laid it across my shoulders, and then put my rugby shirt on. The towel padded out my shoulders nicely. As this proved so successful, I got as many rolled-up socks as I could find and started stuffing them up my sleeves. After this little cosmetic operation I got a load of T-shirts and shoved them up the front. Finally I stuffed a pair of football socks down my crutch and began to strut around like an American Football star.

I didn't look too bad in the mirror, except my National Health goggles spoiled the picture a bit, but I soon fixed that. Without my glasses, my new body looked even more realistic. Being short-sighted was a great help.

I was getting really carried away, strutting and posing, doing a little dodging and weaving, and sparring with the image in the mirror, when Ginny put her head round the door.

'What are you doing, Wayne? You don't half look stupid!'

'Got any better ideas?' I said, and grumpily climbed back into bed.

Chapter 6

Nothing more was said about the suspension, and I spent Thursday evening in my room. By Friday morning my knee was feeling better, and I could move around quite freely.

My mum went out to the doctor's early, because Ginny had developed a rash, and that provided the opportunity I needed to take another look at the shed.

I laid out an old newspaper on the kitchen table, then fetched Jeff's tool-box from the cupboard under the stairs. I opened it up and on a piece of paper made a careful note of where everything was. If I put anything back in the wrong place Jeff would guess I'd been messing about with his tools. I was strictly forbidden to touch anything belonging to Jeff. He kept everything to himself, including the key to the shed, which hung from a clasp attached to his belt.

I selected a screwdriver, a long cold chisel and a hammer. I had about an hour and a half before my mother was due home.

Getting into the shed was a lot easier with a screwdriver. Once inside, I quickly saw that nothing had been changed, except that the oil can was standing to one side of the cut in the floorboard. I was certain I'd put it back over the join, in exactly the place it had been when I'd first noticed the match sticking out from under it. My pulse quickened.

I knelt down hurriedly and soon discovered what I was

looking for. Towards one end of the board there was a bruise and a small dent where something had been inserted into the gap to lever the plank up.

I pushed my steel ruler into the gap, and lined up the cold chisel with the small dent in the plank. I tapped the chisel lightly to ease it down into the join without causing any tell-tale damage. When it was inserted far enough, I steadily pressed my weight on to the cold chisel, bracing it against the ruler, and gently, slowly but surely, levered the board up. It gave way without a protest; the holes around the nails had become slightly enlarged from being used more than once.

I was about to pull the board right out and lay it to one side, when I heard a noise in the garden. Somebody had come round the side of the house.

My heart pounded and the blood pumped around my head, throwing me into total confusion. I froze. Staying quiet was my only hope. If Jeff had come back for something he'd forgotten, I prayed that he'd stay away from the shed. If he noticed the lock, I was done for.

There was silence. I had no time to ease the board back into place. I listened. Nothing.

Then footsteps started down the path. They approached the shed door. The handle rattled. The door opened. Light flooded into the shed.

The man in the doorway visibly jumped when he saw me crouched on the floor. Then he collected himself, and smiled.

'Gawd, son, you didn't half give me a fright!'

It was the postman.

'Can you give this to your father? It's too big to go through the door.'

He held out the parcel so I could take it. I stood up and took it from him.

'Thanks,' I said.

The postman eyed me quizzically, as if to say, 'I've caught you nicking off school, son.'

But instead he said, 'I think I might have heard about you, haven't I?'

I wasn't sure about that, and I certainly didn't recognize him, so I simply said, 'Have you?'

'You must be the villainous Wayne Harding,' he said, beaming as if he'd just worked out the final solution to a crossword puzzle.

'Yes, that's right. How do you know?'

'You go to school with our Sharla. I'm her dad. She's told me all about you. In fact you've acquired quite a reputation in our household recently.'

I was a bit surprised by this piece of information, but it pleased me nevertheless.

'Yes, that's right. I know Sharla.' And then I added, unable to suppress a smile, 'I've been suspended until Monday.'

'Yes, I was sorry to hear about that. If I were to believe half what that girl tells me about that place, well . . .' He paused and let the subject drop, as if further thought on the matter were a waste of time or just likely to make him hopping mad. 'This Mr Smith,' he said indicating the parcel, 'he your stepfather then?'

'That's right,' I replied bitterly. It must have sounded like I really hated him.

'Like that is it?' Sharla's dad replied with a knowing look.

I didn't answer.

Mr Day turned to go.

'Oh well, I'd best be getting along, or else they'll be thinking I've stolen the mail. I'll tell Sharla I saw you. Okay?'

60

'Okay,' I said, once more with a smile.

'Be good! Bye, son.'

Then the shed door closed and his footsteps receded up the path.

The parcel didn't look very interesting. It was a large padded Jiffy envelope. It had a Plymouth postmark. It had been put through the franking machine of Longhurst Garden Supplies, whoever they were.

I put the packet to one side and turned my attention to the hole in the shed floor. Much to my disappointment, there was nothing there. I felt all around the cavity as far as my arm could reach in every direction, but still could find nothing. If anything had been there, it was now gone.

As I pulled my arm out for the final time, I snagged my jumper on the tip of a nail which protruded through the floor. The only way to get my arm out of the hole was to put my other hand in to unhook the sleeve. The operation was a little awkward, but I managed it.

When I examined the offending sleeve, I found a short thread of blue wool stuck to it. The wool must have become detached from the nail when I snagged my arm.

I punched the air and my heart trampolined around inside my ribcage as my imagination began to run away with me. Jeff had been wearing his blue pullover on Monday night! And when had he had that win on the horses and presented us with the sight of two hundred quid? That didn't necessarily mean a thing; he often wore it when he came in from work. But these thoughts could do nothing to calm my excitement. If only I could prove he was mixed up in something he shouldn't be; if only I could get something on him!

I put the floorboard back into position and hammered the nails into place. I left everything as it was, screwed the lock back on to the door and returned the tools to the house, where I laid them carefully back in the tool-box. When I'd put the tool-box away, I went upstairs to my mum's bedroom.

Creeping into your mum's bedroom when you're not supposed to gives you a disturbing sort of feeling, like going into an empty church and pinching prayer books. The clean smell of the room was pronounced, an almost overwhelming mixture of furniture polish and perfume. All of a sudden my shoes felt very muddy, and I became anxious about leaving marks in the thick pile of the carpet.

I held my breath and tip-toed over to the chest of drawers. The weak sun filtered into the room through the net curtains and showed up the dust on all the surfaces.

I eased open the drawers silently, and began lifting up the neat piles of clothing, looking for Jeff's pullover.

The first drawer contained underwear, and in the corner was a packet of condoms. The discovery held me fascinated for a second, then I closed the drawer quickly and started on the next, imagining my mother would come back at any time, catching me fingering the small secrets of her private life. The thought made me shudder.

The second drawer contained shirts. At the top of the third was the blue pullover. I pulled it out and unfolded it on the bed, where I examined the sleeves. I couldn't be sure at first, but when I held the sleeve of the right arm up to the light and poked my finger inside, I could see that it was definitely snagged.

So it seemed that Jeff could have been in the shed last night, and if he had, what had he taken?

I laid the pullover carefully back in the drawer and pushed it gently to. Jeff wouldn't notice that it had been removed; it was my mother who folded and put away all the clothes in our house.

I put the kettle on when I got back downstairs, and my mum and Ginny arrived home just in time for coffee. They seemed pleased to see me, and Ginny was full of the conversation she'd had with the doctor about her rash. She told me all about going shopping on the way back, but I wasn't concentrating, because it's hard to listen when you've just remembered you've left a parcel locked up in the shed.

For the rest of the day I felt like a prisoner. I helped around the house and played with Ginny in the afternoon. There was simply no opportunity to sneak out to the shed.

Jeff asked about the post as soon as he got in, and for a fleeting moment seemed agitated when my mum told him that the postman hadn't been. Then he interrogated me in the kitchen after tea about the time that my mum and Ginny were out at the doctor's. I gave him the same negative reply.

Something was working Jeff up into a foul mood and there was nothing I had done which could have been responsible for it. Surely it couldn't be that package Mr Day had delivered? Seed catalogues didn't seem much to get steamed up about.

He began to shout at me again. 'If you're fit enough to be up, you're fit enough to be out. I don't want you hanging around again tonight!'

If I was kicked out there would be little hope of breaking back into the shed. I thought quickly. I took a deep breath and gambled. Jeff had a soft spot for Ginny.

'Look', I said, fixing Jeff in the eye and holding his gaze. 'I can't walk far on my knee. Do you think I could use the shed tonight?' He was visibly taken aback. I didn't usually make requests. My mother looked at him expectantly, and he wasn't quite sure which way to turn.

'I don't know. I mean what do you want to use the shed for?'

I had my answer ready.

'Look, it's a bit difficult,' I said, nodding towards Ginny, who was undressing her doll on the kitchen table.

My mother cottoned on and saved the day. She took Ginny's hand and led her out of the room, saying she could watch some cartoons on the video.

I gripped the back of a chair, more for moral support than anything else, and continued, 'I want to make something for Ginny's birthday. I thought, perhaps, as I can't walk very well, I might be able to use the shed.'

'Oh?' he said, sounding quite interested. He treated Ginny as if she was his own daughter. 'What do you want to make?'

By now I'd got the idea fully formed in my mind.

'I want to make a puppet. You know, one with strings. All I need is a few scraps of plywood and a fret saw. I'll make the joints with paper fasteners. I can get those from Frocesters' when I collect the papers. I'll be fit to start again tomorrow.'

My mum came back into the room and before Jeff could reply she said, 'Go on, Jeff, just this once. It's freezing cold out.'

Jeff relented reluctantly and took the key off his belt.

'Just you be careful,' he said. 'The saw's hanging up in the cupboard and there's off-cuts under the work-bench. Oh, and you'd better take some matches to light the stove. I'll be out later to see what you're doing, so make sure you get on with it. If you don't get it finished, you'll have to do the rest at school.'

'Thanks, Jeff!' I said, and tried to be as cool as possible as I went about my preparations.

*

64

As soon as I closed the shed door behind me, I grabbed the parcel off the bench and shoved it up my jumper. I held it secure by wedging the bottom end into the top of my trousers. Its bulk made moving a bit difficult, but if Jeff commented on it, I'd just say I'd got gutache.

I lit the stove and started sifting through all the odd lengths of wood which were stacked under the bench. I found some solid pieces for the head and body of the puppet, and a collection of suitable strips of plywood for the limbs.

I only had a vague idea how to make it, but I had to make a reasonable effort, or else Jeff would think I'd been playing him up.

I'd barely finished cutting out all the limb sections when Jeff poked his nose round the door. He stood in the doorway letting all the cold air in. He smoked for a minute, taking it all in before he said anything. I worked on self-consciously. He was sizing me up. When he eventually spoke, he spoke gruffly.

'Here, let's have a look?'

I cleared a space on the bench and spread the pieces out. He shoved me out of the way and examined my work more closely.

'Looks a bit like a road accident at the moment, don't it?' he said with a smirk, but not without a touch of warmth. 'It'll be okay when it's put together. I didn't know you had it in you, Wayne.'

No, you don't know much about me, I thought resentfully.

'A bit of paint and it'll come up fine,' he continued. 'Ginny will like it. What are you going to use for the strings?'

'Dunno. Fishing line, maybe. What do you think?' I said.

A sensible conversation with Jeff was a rare thing, but I didn't want to prolong it any longer than necessary because the parcel was beginning to burn a hole in its hiding place.

'Fishing line, you say? Sounds possible. I'll give it some thought.'

He didn't sound at all dismissive. On the contrary, he seemed quite interested in the project.

'Look, you can stay out a bit longer if you like. Stay out till nine. I'm off down the pub, so make sure you lock up before you go back in.'

'Yeah, well, thanks,' I said.

I went back to work, happy at this turn of events, which had come right out of the blue through a stroke of genius on my part. Cool as a confidence trickster, I'd got away with it, parcel stuffed up my jumper the whole time and all. I was making progress.

By nine o'clock I'd got the different bits of the puppet sanded down and ready for painting. All I had left to do then was drill a few holes in the right places and put the thing together. I'd even found time to make the cross-piece to control the strings. I packed the pieces up and stuffed them into my coat pockets.

I'd learned my lessons the hard way, and I wasn't going to get too cocky. I didn't trust Jeff. He might say he was going to the pub, but I wasn't about to take any chances.

I'd been thinking about the packet. I had two choices. I could smuggle it up to my room and then place it on the front step after Sharla's dad delivered in the morning, or I could intercept him on his round before he got to our house and give the parcel back. It would be delivered as if nothing untoward had ever happened.

The first option was far too risky. I couldn't guarantee that Jeff would be out of the way when the post arrived,

66

nor could I be certain that I could carry the parcel to and from my bedroom without it being detected. The dim light of the shed had offered me some protection; getting through the kitchen and up the stairs was a different proposition. I had to get rid of the packet, at least temporarily.

I switched off the light and opened the shed door a crack, so I could see out. I waited for my eyes to adjust to the dark and listened carefully. I could see that the kitchen light was out, and that presented a worry. There was no way of telling if Jeff was lurking in there, ready to find fault if I didn't finish in time. It was a risk I had to take.

Our neighbours had a concrete coal bunker. It was attached to the wall of the house, adjacent to the wire fence which divided the gardens. I had decided to dump the parcel up the opening of the coal bunker. It would be safe and it would stay dry if it rained. If Mr Richardson was working nights like I thought, then it should be all right.

Depositing the parcel meant only a short detour across the grass, and I wouldn't have to take it from under my jumper until the last minute.

There was already a frost on the ground, and the grass crackled under my feet as I stole across the garden to the fence. I eased the package out of the waistband of my trousers and laid it carefully in the opening of the bunker. A weight fell off me, and I stood up.

No sooner had I done so than Jeff came round the side of the house. I pressed myself into the wall, and held my breath.

He stopped and lit a cigarette. Harsh shadows remoulded his face, making him ugly. Then the match flickered out.

At first I thought I was in the clear, but then he said, accusingly, 'What are you doing? I thought I told you to go straight back in when you'd finished.'

By making a conscious effort I managed to keep my voice under control. 'I thought I heard one of next door's rabbits scuffling about in the garden, but I must have been mistaken. You can see them in the cage. Look.'

The cage was on the path on the other side of the coal bunker. I could see quite clearly that it was locked. It was a cold night to be sleeping in a hutch.

'I don't want to look. Come here and give us the key.'

Before I got really close to him I could smell the beer and fags on him. I handed over the key, and made to move round him, but before I could pass he clipped me round the head with the back of his hand; he always found it hard to resist when my mother wasn't around.

Back in the kitchen he was more reasonable again. My mum busied herself making coffee, and I showed Jeff what I'd done on the puppet since he'd left. Through his boozy haze he seemed quite impressed.

'Here's a couple of quid,' he said. 'Get some paints.'

I didn't get much sleep that night. When next door's garden light went on I nearly had a fit and leapt to the window. It was only Mrs Richardson letting the cat in.

The hours passed slowly. I heard my mum and Jeff come upstairs. Then their bed began to creak and I tried not to listen. I thought a lot about Sharla, but she was not a comfort; she just kept me awake. I puzzled over ways of gaining entry into the glasshouse, and by one o'clock I had worked out a plan. Some time between two and three my body tricked me into sleep, but by five-thirty I was wide awake again. I got out of bed and messed about with the puppet I was making for Ginny. I formed plans for dressing it up like the Pied Piper. I designed a hat and cloak.

At half past six the house was still quiet, and I left as usual to do my paper round. As it was Saturday, Mum and Jeff wouldn't stir until nine o'clock. I never ate breakfast before going out, and certainly this morning I wouldn't have been able to summon up an appetite even if they'd helicoptered egg and bacon in from the Ritz.

I crept silently along the back of the house and hopped over the low wire fence. The packet was where I had left it; it felt only slightly damp. It was no more mucky than it would have been had it come straight out of Mr Day's bag.

I stuffed the packet down my trousers and, thinking I was about to take no chances, I left to go round the side of Mr Richardson's house, when I walked straight into Mr Richardson coming home from night shift.

Mr Richardson looked at me curiously.

'You usually trample through other people's back yards, Wayne? Eh?' he asked grumpily, uncertain whether to start a row or hurry in to bed.

'Sorry,' I said, hoping to forestall his anger, 'I was just looking at your rabbits. I hope you don't mind. I wasn't up to anything, honest.'

'No, I don't suppose you were,' said Mr Richardson ambiguously. He was weary and, luckily for me, had chosen to go straight to bed. 'Next time, use your own passage, Wayne.'

'Sorry,' I said, as he squeezed by and continued round to the back door.

After I'd been to Frocesters' to do my paper round I had a little time to kill before Mr Day was due to come our way. I sat on the kerb close to Patel's, so I'd be safe from Hovis, but I doubted very much whether he'd be up that early. Patel's is the corner shop just down the street from us. It sells everything from magazines to galvanized buckets. It opens all hours, and every day of the week. Everyone round our way calls it the Paki Shop. Most people say they hate the Patels, but there's always a long queue in there on Sundays. I'd like to do my paper round from there, because it's nearer home, but there's a big waiting list.

I did some sorting out for little Sally and Stewart, the Patel twins, once. That's why Hovis sometimes calls me Paki Lover.

From Patel's I could also keep a look-out for Mr Day coming up the road. I wasn't sure which way he would come. My mum's bedroom overlooks the street, so I stayed close behind a parked car.

It was a cold and boring wait. The temptation to take the packet out of the top of my trousers and give it the once over was irresistible.

It was an ordinary Jiffy bag, and the padding made it difficult to work out exactly what was inside. The contents seemed to be divided into three smaller parts, so the packet had an articulated feel. The three parts were quite thick. My earlier impression that it was probably seed catalogues, and maybe even a free offer, didn't seem to be far from the truth. But short of removing the staples from the Jiffy bag, I couldn't really settle the question, so I shoved it back down my trousers and waited.

When Mr Day arrived on the scene, he came suddenly. I didn't see him until he was five doors down from my house. There was little point doing anything dramatic, like crawling commando-style down the gutter to avoid being seen. If Jeff just happened to be looking out for the post and saw me cavorting on my hands and knees I'd cop it; anyway Mr Day would reach our house long before I got to him.

I stood up and walked quickly towards the house next door but one to mine. I shot down the side passage and waited. Sure enough Mr Day came down the path of the house next door to that.

'Mr Day!' I hissed. 'Mr Day!'

He stopped half-way along the path. He was about to greet me heartily, but mercifully he realized that my exaggerated whisper and frantic gestures meant that I wanted him to come over for a quiet word.

'Hello, son,' he said as he came over to the fence. 'What are you doing here then? I thought you lived a couple of doors down.'

'I do, but I had to see you before you got to our house. It's about that package you delivered yesterday . . . it's a bit awkward really.'

'Well, don't be shy,' he said kindly. 'Come on, out with it!'

He glanced anxiously up at the window above me. I climbed over the fence and joined him.

'Well,' I said, 'it's like this. I've still got the package and I'd like to give it back to you so you can deliver it again.'

It was a relief to have said it.

'Oh, I see,' he said with a chuckle.

I wondered whether he did.

'Will you take it back then?' I asked anxiously.

'What? You mean interfere with the Royal Mail?' he said in a shocked tone of voice. 'Why the very idea is outrageous!'

By the way he exaggerated the last word, I knew, thankfully, that he wasn't serious. I looked at him, still hoping.

'Why, of course I will,' he said at last. 'Anything to

oblige a friend of Sharla's. You mustn't tell anyone, mind, else there'll be trouble.'

'Thanks, thanks,' I said, as I slipped him the Jiffy bag. I was getting tired of wearing it down my trousers; it pinched in all the wrong places.

'All right now? I guess you must be quite relieved. Don't worry, I'm not going to ask you all about it. You must have your reasons.'

'Yes,' I said.

'And anyway, I can't hang around all day. I've got to deliver these to this house here, so you just take a head start. I'll go the long way round to the next couple of houses, and by the time I get to yours you'll be safely in. Piece of cake. Now hop it before we both get done for loitering with intent to interfere with the mail!'

I set off down the path and when I was safely into the road Mr Day shouted, 'Oh, by the way, Sharla says she'll see you on Monday!'

For once I returned home with a smile on my face.

Jeff was in the lounge when I got back. He was up earlier than usual for a Saturday; my mum, bleary-eyed, was making breakfast in the kitchen.

She gave me a mug of tea to take through to Jeff. I was half-way down the hall when Mr Day knocked on the door. Jeff was out in an instant to open the door, and took the package straight upstairs. The expression on his face told me he was a man who needed some time alone and didn't want to be disturbed.

It was a puzzle, but at least he was out of my hair. So I turned cheerfully back to the kitchen, and there, with a smirk on my face, I devoured his egg, bacon and sausage with three slices of fried bread, and took great delight in slurping down his tea!

Chapter 7

When I left the house after my hearty breakfast I strolled away from the estate with the satisfaction of a man who had eaten well and felt a little more in command of himself. I followed the main road in the direction of school, intent on making a further exploration of the glasshouse.

The pavement was narrow, and heavy lorries thundered past, perilously close. The old brick terraces fronted straight on to the pavement. Their walls and windows were covered in grime thrown up from the road. As a pedestrian, you risked life and limb with the big wheels rolling by at eye level. This noisy and smelly ordeal lasted for a few hundred yards, and then the road widened. Large houses lined the far side of the road, interspersed by small meadows leading down to the canal, and on the other side of the road were small industrial units, hiding optimistically behind ancient privet hedges and scanty screens of poplar saplings.

The scrapyard was situated half-way along, next to the petrol station. It was bounded by a high corrugated fence with coils of barbed wire scrolled across the top. I turned right at the scrapyard, down a narrow cut between the fence and the filling station. This alleyway eventually opened up on to a track which met it at right angles. The track must have been a proper road once, but it had gone to holes, and vegetation had filled all the cracks in the tarmac. It was the sort of track which filled up with muddy water whenever it rained.

The track was in fact a cul-de-sac, and at the blind end stood the house I had seen from the glasshouse the night before. It was an enormous Victorian villa, four storeys high, slightly taller than it was wide. The big windows on the ground floor were boarded up with corrugated iron. The front door was criss-crossed with planks, barring entry. The upstairs windows were heavily masked by peeling shutters.

On both sides of the house a high brick wall shut off the garden from view. There was a heavy door set in the wall on the left-hand side.

I followed the track for a short distance away from the house, and found that it curved away through a tunnel under the railway line, before following the slope of the hill to join the road which ran around the estate of private houses.

The tunnel was damp and musty. It smelt vaguely of urine. The floor was littered with beer cans. It gave me the creeps, so I went back to have another look at the house.

House martins had nested under the eaves at some time in the past, but this was the only sign of occupation.

There was work going on in the scrapyard and its noise drowned out any sounds coming from the garden. I opened the front gate and followed the path through the small garden. I tried the door in the wall. The latch was stiff, and when it finally gave it cracked like a gun going off. I waited for a moment, listening, before pushing it open. There was nothing to see but the side of the house with its rusty fire escape and network of drainpipes running at all angles across the wall.

I closed the gate and crouched in the dark recesses of the fire escape until I felt safe to go on.

From the corner of the house, I could see to my right a terrace ringed by stone urns sprouting ragged clumps of heather. Beyond the terrace the railway line was clearly visible. I could see the spot where I'd tumbled down the embankment. Neat lawns stretched away from the terrace, but the surrounding borders were unkempt. At the bottom of this vast garden was the glasshouse. The lights were on, and an old man was moving around inside.

I watched for a while from the safety of the house. Once again the aroma of tobacco drifted across the garden. A train rattled past, and the sun came out. The old man in the glasshouse looked harmless enough. He appeared happy in his work.

Last night I had decided that, rather than be caught skulking about, it would be better if I made a direct approach. If I was to gain entry, then I needed to be bold. I had rehearsed my lines. The thought of wandering the streets at night, prey to the cold and to the likes of Hovis, stiffened my resolve. Nevertheless, my palms still sweated as I walked down the gravel path.

The old man disappeared from view, but I could hear him moving things about on the metal staging.

I knocked on the door, practising what I was going to say. My mind raced; I was learning to live on my wits.

There was no response to my knock.

I knocked again more loudly.

There was still no reply.

I was in two minds whether to poke my head inside, or give up and run away, when the old man suddenly appeared in the doorway.

He didn't seem to be of this world. He was very tanned and his face was dried up like an old prune. His jaw was unshaven, and the white stubble under his lip was stained yellow with nicotine. He wore heavy trousers, held up by a broad leather belt which might have been borrowed from a carthorse. The Fair Isle pullover was badly holed, but his collarless white shirt had been immaculately laundered, starched and pressed. Someone obviously looked after him.

He eyed me suspiciously, and pushed his straw hat back on his forehead.

'Yes? What do you want?' he said, as if I'd just interrupted something very important.

'I've come about the job,' I stammered, hopping from toe to toe and looking rather too sheepish.

'Sorry?' he said, waiting for me to explain.

'I've come about the advertisement in the post office,' I explained.

'What advertisement is that then?'

'The one for the Saturday job. You know, six hours gardening, some greenhouse work. Suitable for teenager,' I went on hopefully.

'You've got the wrong place then, I'm afraid. There's no jobs here.'

He smiled kindly, but made no move to invite me inside. In fact he positively blocked the door so I couldn't see in past the plants which masked the interior.

Having come this far, I wasn't about to give up.

'Isn't this Aubretia Villas?' I asked, squinting at him through my glasses and faking a puzzled look. I pushed my glasses off the bridge of my nose to give the impression of being very confused. 'I noticed some bits of aubretia in the front garden, so I thought this must be it. The card in the window said it was by the garage on the main road.'

The old man listened patiently, but I was unsure whether he was convinced.

'Like I said, I'm afraid you must have got the wrong

76

place. This isn't Aubretia Villas. There's certainly no place like that around here.'

'Oh,' I said, sounding defeated. I looked at the garden, as if to say, Well, I would have loved the opportunity to work here.

The old man followed my gaze, and something in his expression told me he couldn't help but be reminded of how neglected the herbaceous borders had become; the kitchen garden was a tangle of weeds.

'I just thought,' I continued, 'that this must be it, seeing as how overrun things are here. I was really looking forward to taking on this sort of job. I like a challenge.'

'Ah, a fellow after my own heart,' said the old man, wistfully and to no one in particular.

I pressed home my point.

'I'd like to get into gardening when I leave school. It isn't the money that I want so much at the moment, as the experience.'

The old man relit his pipe and looked at me quizzically through a rising cloud of blue smoke.

'Go on, son,' he said, 'I'm still listening.'

I turned to look at the garden again and then I said, 'We've only got a small garden at home and my stepdad won't let me do anything in it. It's hopeless.'

'What about school then, haven't they got a patch there?'

'Yes, but I'm too brainy to be in the gardening group, so I never get a chance.'

I'd run out of steam. There was nothing else I could say. I hadn't told the truth and I felt guilty about it. It was okay to lie at school. Everybody expected it and everybody did it, but it didn't seem right in the present situation. In the circumstances I decided it would perhaps be best if I just went away after all.

'Sorry to bother you,' I said, and turned to go, but before I could make a move the old man caught me by the shoulder.

'Hang on, hang on. Hold your horses. You're a lousy liar, you know, which suggests to me that you're an honest lad at heart. But now you're here and have gone to all the trouble of concocting this elaborate story, you may as well come in, have a cup of tea and tell me some more. Things have been a bit lonely round here lately, as it happens.'

The old man stepped aside and waved me through the door.

'I'm Tom,' he said, holding out his hand.

'Wayne', I said, and shook his hand. It was strong but had the warmth of a hug.

'Come in then, Wayne, come in. Tell me what you think.'

It was wonderful, better than I ever imagined it would be. The glasshouse was incredibly light inside. It gave you the strange feeling of being outside and indoors at the same time. It bewildered the senses. The sky, seen through the glass, looked very cold and forbidding, yet the air in the glasshouse was warm and remote from winter; it was like being transported in a bubble of summer. Such a structure should have been frail, segmented as it was into panes which occasionally creaked in the breeze. When I craned my neck back to stare upwards, I was presented with an illusion of something collapsing ever so slowly and my head was filled with a premonition of the whole thing crashing down. But the construction was incredibly strong; the cedar framework held everything rigid, and the brickwork had rooted the whole structure firmly into the earth and raised it towards the sky, and there it belonged, of both, and suspended between the two. We had done the four elements in English at school, and I knew when I stepped into the glasshouse with Tom that the glasshouse was to do with them all. There was fire and water there too. Feelings are strange and private; they are difficult to describe. I felt all this in a shiver that ran down my spine.

I felt as insubstantial as a ghost as Tom led me down the central aisle, under the pale lights which compensated for the absence of the weak February sunshine.

'Oh, by the way, this is Carlos,' said Tom as we reached the bench at the far end of the glasshouse.

'Sorry,' I said, a little baffled as I could see no one else present. Then I thought he must be referring to a cat, only there was no cat in sight.

Tom sat down next to a tall plant with dense green foliage. He offered me a seat.

'Carlos,' he said, gesturing behind him. 'Carlos, meet Wayne.'

I looked under the bench, but I still couldn't see any sign of a cat. I was uncertain how to respond, so I simply went along with whatever game he was playing and said, 'Hello Carlos, nice to meet you!'

Tom grinned; he was obviously pleased by my response.

'I'm glad you take to plants . . . Yes, I can see you are a man after my own heart. Not many lads are interested these days. All they want is girls and ghetto blasters. That's right, isn't it, Wayne?'

'Right,' I said, still unable to understand who Carlos was. Then suddenly I had an inspiration. I decided to hazard a guess.

'What sort of plant is Carlos exactly?' I asked hopefully. 'I've never seen one quite like him before.'

The look on Tom's face told me I had said the right thing.

'Ah, good. For a minute, I thought you were thinking I was right off my trolley,' he said, dissolving into laughter, 'introducing somebody who wasn't there! Carlos? What sort of plant is he? Banana plant. Carlos gives two bunches a year, no more and no less. Never fails. Wrong time of the year at the moment. He doesn't like winter.'

'Do all your plants have names?' I asked, warming to the conversation and discovering that I did after all have at least a little curiosity about plants, particularly if they were plants with crazy names.

'No, only the ones I know personally,' Tom replied. 'Like old Wily Willie, that variegated ivy over there. And Chalky, that rather anaemic cheese plant across the way. I can't bear the thought of throwing him out.'

Perhaps he was really off his trolley after all.

'Plants are generally better company than people,' he continued wistfully, 'present company excepted, of course. They don't get on your wick like people do. Well, not often, anyroad. Don't you agree?'

Having had my sort of experience with people, I was inclined to agree.

'Yes, it often seems like that,' I said.

Tom looked me up and down. He scratched his head and thought for a moment. Then he leant back towards the banana plant as if to consult it about an issue of some substance. After a moment's silence, he spoke quietly and slowly, so his words were just distinct above the whisper of the fans.

'It's decided then; we'll make a deal.'

'I beg your pardon?' I said, confused by this change of tack.

'It's a deal,' he repeated, holding out his hand. 'You

80

can start today if you like. I need some more help around here. I can't pay you, mind. Mrs Philpot wouldn't run to that. In fact, she'd better not find out, or else I'll be in big trouble.'

'Brilliant!' I exclaimed, excited by this turn of events. 'But who's Mrs Philpot?'

'The Boss!' he said dramatically. 'But I'll tell you about her later. First, we'll make some tea and confirm the deal.'

That was how I met Tom, and came to work at the glasshouse.

Tom warmed to me as the morning wore on, and he began to tell me a number of things. He kept on about how he was seventy-four years old and still going strong. He said it was the outdoor life and getting up early. He insisted he was seventy-four and didn't look a day over sixty. I hadn't the heart to tell him that my first impression of him had been of a man of eighty.

Tom had a bad cough, which rattled in his throat like an angry flue-pipe. It would double him up occasionally, as he was talking fast and furiously. Tom liked to stay physically active, but every time he strained with a sack of peat, I thought he'd bust a blood vessel or have a heart attack.

Tom was a retired farm hand who'd moved back into town when the tied cottage he'd lived in for forty years was given over to a younger man and his family.

This momentous upheaval he accepted as part of the natural pattern of his life. According to his way of thinking there was justice in it, but I couldn't see it.

Now he lived in a small council flat on the other side of town, with his wife, whom he always referred to as his 'missus'. When he retired he came to work for Mrs

Philpot, a strange lady if ever there was one. Her father, who had been a mill owner, had left her the house and the remainder of his fortune, much of which he'd lost in the depression of the 1930s. It was Mr Fletcher, Mrs Philpot's father, who built the glasshouse. His passion had been the cultivation of orchids.

Alice Fletcher was no delicate hot-house bloom herself. She'd grown wild in her late teens and run away with a farm boy who had been killed in a farming accident shortly afterwards, but not before he had made her Alice Philpot.

It was a brief childless marriage and, following the accident, Mr Fletcher, who was now widowed himself, took Alice back into his house. She never remarried.

Her father died before the outbreak of the Second World War. The thought of Hitler getting at his orchids was too much for him. Alice stayed on in the house, continuing her father's love of exotic flowers.

She'd been living in the same house all those years, until six months ago, when she suffered a minor stroke and had retired under duress to a nursing home.

She had lived seeing virtually no one for all that time, until Tom turned up one day. He was motorcycling round the neighbourhood looking for a garden to do up. Deprived of the land he had worked on for over forty years, he needed a patch of earth to plant his boots in. That had been nine years ago.

It seemed Alice Philpot had recognized something of her dead husband in Tom, and after a little persuasion she took him on, for no pay, of course, because Tom wasn't the sort to make demands, and anyway, as Mrs Philpot explained, she couldn't afford it.

Alice Philpot wanted Tom to do the garden while she devoted all her energies to her project in the glasshouse.

'So for nine years,' as Tom put it, 'I've been having this affair with Mrs Philpot, and you're the first to know about it!'

I was quite shocked. I wasn't sure about people having affairs, and I certainly thought Tom was too old.

'Why are you telling me all this? Doesn't your wife know?' I sounded quite surprised.

'Ah, yes. She knows about Mrs Philpot, and she doesn't mind.'

Tom noticed my jaw drop open at this latest snippet of information.

'She doesn't mind, because she doesn't think I've got the stuff in me any more, so it can do no harm. She's right and all!' Tom laughed. 'You look so shocked!'

He began to giggle twice as hysterically as Becca and Sharla, but then, just as suddenly, this turned into a nasty fit of coughing and I had to fetch him a cup of water so he could recover himself.

'Thanks,' he said, wiping the spittle from his lips. 'Oh yes, me missus knows all right.' Then he added mysteriously, 'But she doesn't know about the project. No one does.'

'What project's that then?' I asked. 'And why are you telling me?'

'Ah, now you have it,' he said with a sad smile. 'Perhaps I've said too much, and I haven't told you nearly the half of it yet. Some bits I'm not even sure I know! This place has a special atmosphere all of its own; something to do with all that concentrated growing, I reckon.'

He looked around at the staging stacked with pots, and then let his gaze float beneath the huge framework of wood and glass.

And what was Alice Philpot's project? He wouldn't tell me just then.

But though he wasn't prepared to answer my question, he did offer me a clue to why he had allowed me to enter at least some way into Alice Philpot's secret realm.

'You have an honest look to your face,' he said.

The morning passed quickly, and at twelve-thirty, Tom said, 'Well, that's enough work for today, young Wayne. I've got to be off home for my dinner.'

We hadn't done much except shift a few sacks about, chatter and drink tea, so if this was work I was all in favour of it.

'Come back tomorrow,' he said, 'at nine. What do you say?'

'Thanks,' I said, 'I will.'

Nothing was going to stop me.

Tom picked up his crash helmet from under the staging, and strapped it on. From that moment, conversation was impossible. Like a diver under water, Tom gestured that we should leave and lock up.

Outside the glasshouse I waited while he wheeled his ancient Triumph motorbike on to the path. He unravelled the padlock chain and climbed aboard the machine. Then he kicked it into life; like its rider, it was surprisingly healthy.

'Want a lift?' he said pointing to a small pithy helmet dangling from the pillion. 'It belongs to me missus. It should fit you.'

'No thanks, I'll walk,' I said.

'What?'

'I'll walk! Thanks!' I shouted, and followed him up the path.

When we reached the wall at the top end of the garden, I held the door open while he manoeuvred the bike through. He handed me the key and I locked up. When

I'd passed it back to him, he shook my hand again.

'See you tomorrow!' he shouted cheerily above the noise of the engine.

'Bye,' I replied, and Tom roared off down the track to the tunnel under the railway line.

I stood for a moment and imagined Mrs Philpot alone in that vast house. I wondered how she had managed to survive through all those winters, through all those years since her father died, with no one to talk to except her orchids. But then, as Tom said, perhaps plants were better company than people.

I was fifteen minutes late for lunch. Jeff took it out on me immediately.

'Your mother has spent the last hour getting your dinner ready, and you can't even be bothered to get here on time. Where've you been?'

He scowled over his empty plate.

Ginny averted her eyes and stabbed at a sausage with her fork. I wondered whether it was me or Jeff she was pretending to stick it into.

'Where've you been?' he said, mopping up brown sauce with a piece of bread. My mother looked petrified as usual. Why didn't she leave him? The money, I supposed.

'Out,' I said sullenly.

'Don't be cheeky to your father!'

My mother, in her own way, was trying to calm the situation, but she misjudged my mood. I'd come back from somewhere I'd been made welcome. I didn't need them. Not at this minute anyway. I had somewhere else to go.

'He's not my father,' I said bitterly.

Jeff rose from the table, pushing it out of his way. It made a terrifying screeching sound, like someone having a tooth pulled out with rusty pliers. He picked up his plate and flung it towards the sink. It exploded off the taps. Ginny ducked. The shattered pieces hurtled about. A sliver stung my face, making it bleed, another lodged in Ginny's hair. She screamed, and my mother quickly bundled her out of the room.

Jeff was white with rage. I couldn't move.

'Pick that up!' he shouted, gesturing at the fragments of china littering the kitchen floor.

I went to get the dustpan and brush from the pantry, but he snatched it out of my hands and flung it into the hall.

'Not with that,' he snapped. 'Use your hands. If I'm not your father, then you're not my son. If you're not my son, I don't have to provide for you. I don't have to provide you with anything. I don't have to provide dinner!'

With that, he took my lunch out of the oven and began to eat, while I picked the pieces off the floor. He was a messy eater. He had a mouth like a dustcart. The table around his plate was spattered with gobs of brown sauce and congealed fat; he'd turn any table into a tip.

When I'd finished clearing up, I had to wash up, and then I was confined to my room. So much for my vision of power, and so much for slaying the Hell Snakes of Steel. So much for the safety of the glasshouse. Right now it seemed like I was right back where I started.

Chapter 8

I felt restless again that night, in the way that you do in midsummer when you're a kid and it's still light outside, and you can't sleep for the heat and all the things still going on beyond the drawn curtains. But I was no longer just a kid and it was still winter out there.

I lay on my back thinking about Sharla, though not so much thinking about her as wondering how to keep her in my mind and out of it at the same time. I wanted to think about her, because I was beginning to see how much I liked her and, if I was really honest, fancied her. But I didn't want to think about her, too, because the whole thing was impossible. Sharla read all those photo-strip magazines and romantic novels, and I was nothing like anybody in them. It seemed hopeless and that kept me awake. I'd never seen her in this romantic light before, but since that business in the bogs with Hovis and my encounter with her father, she'd not been out of my mind for long. She had invaded some of those spaces in my imagination which had been reserved for childish fantasies. I had no experience of girls, and I wasn't exactly inundated with offers, not even from First Years. I was busting to tell her all about what had happened. I wanted to tell her about the glasshouse, but Tom had sworn me to secrecy.

I dreamt about a life with Sharla in the glasshouse. There was no chromium hall like I had imagined before, when I lay in bed nursing my knee, no huge silver screen;

just me and Sharla, sunshine and plants. But as I've said, it was all idle fancy, and in the end it just made me sad.

It must have been in the early hours of Sunday morning when I woke from some such futile dream; I'd heard my mum and Jeff go to bed long before. The sound of footsteps outside the house had brought me abruptly back to reality.

The footsteps were stealthy. They stopped every now and then. Someone was creeping round outside the house. I knelt up in bed, eased one corner of the curtain carefully aside, and peered down into the garden. I could see nothing and no one. Sometimes foxes came down from the railway embankment to raid the dustbins.

Then I heard a faint, but familiar rattle. Someone was trying the door of the shed. I could just make out a shadowy form bent over the lock. Whoever it was, was having difficulty getting it undone. It wasn't Jeff. After a moment more they gave up the struggle.

When the intruder turned round, he stood up straight and stared up at my window. It was Hovis.

I ducked away from the window in a flash, my pulse pounding. When I looked again, he was gone.

What I'd seen made no sense. I played the incident over and over in my head. I was certain that Hovis knew I was watching from behind the curtains.

I lay facing the door, expecting to hear his fatal footfall on the stairs. I lay awake for a long time. He never came.

When I went downstairs to do my Sunday papers, there was a crumpled note on the mat. I picked it up. It was written on a page torn out of a school exercise book. I hoped in vain that it might be from Sharla, saying she'd missed me and was looking forward to my return to school. I unfolded the paper. It said: 'SEE YOU MONDAY',

88

and was written in Hovis's scrawl. I screwed it up and stuffed it into my pocket. It was just the kind of message calculated to cheer me up. Just one more thing to look forward to!

At ten o'clock I was back at Mrs Philpot's. As I approached the terrace, I could see Tom rubbing furiously at the side of the glasshouse. He was obviously in a grim mood, and I wasn't sure how he was going to respond to my arrival. Yesterday's welcome suddenly seemed too good to be true.

As I went down the path I could see that there was something very wrong. The glass had been daubed with red paint. The letters were nearly a foot high, spelling out a clear message:

THIS IS YOUR LAST CHAN

Tom obviously had his enemies too. He had already set to work with paint stripper on the last word, and had got rid of two letters, but the message was still clear. Rivulets of red paint dribbled down from each letter. The whole thing was a mess.

Tom swung round, startled, when I came up behind him. Seeing that it was me, he relaxed.

'Right bloody mess isn't it?' he said. 'Who do you reckon would do a thing like this then?'

'I don't know,' I said, not realizing he was asking a rhetorical question.

'Well, I can tell you, but I can't prove it.' Tom scowled in the direction of the scrapyard. 'Came over that wall I reckon.'

'Did anybody see them, do you think?' I asked.

'What, round here? You've got to be joking. There's nobody round here at night.'

'How do you know they came over that wall then?' I asked.

'I just know, that's all,' said Tom. 'Here, grab a cloth.'

He reached into his trouser pocket and pulled out an old dishcloth.

'You'll need some gloves. This stripper's foul stuff. Carlos will give you the gloves.' Tom still had his sense of humour.

I went into the glasshouse. I felt quite at home there; everything had already begun to feel familiar. I found the gloves under the staging next to the banana plant.

'Morning, Carlos!' I said breezily, and stroked a big leaf lightly with the palm of my hand. I was about to go back out to join Tom when I realized there was somebody else outside. I waited, hidden by some tall plants. I thought the visitor might be a friend of Mrs Philpot. Whoever it was might tell her about me, and then Tom would be in trouble.

I couldn't see much of the visitor, but I caught a glimpse of his face. He was smiling and seemed pleasant enough. The man was showing an obvious concern for what had happened to the glass, but Tom answered him icily, speaking in a tone of voice very different from the one with which he had greeted me when I had arrived the day before. And he showed no sign of softening.

Eventually, the man left. When I heard the garden door close, I came out.

'Who was that?' I said to Tom, who had already resumed work on the glass.

'Him?' He paused, and spat on the ground. 'Jarvis, the scrap-metal merchant. You did well to stay away from him.'

'Why's that then? He seemed pleasant enough to me.'

Tom looked at me sorrowfully, as if I'd just admitted

buying the Eiffel Tower from a shady French estate agent.

'That's what they all think, especially the council. He's as hard as nails, and twice as slimy as a toad in butter. Mr Smartarse Jarvis would rob his own grandmother. He's a twister, and if I could prove he did this piece of work here, I'd have him.'

Tom was working himself up into a purple rage and had to sit down on his smoking chair by the door to catch his breath.

'You mean you think he did it?' I said.

'I don't think it, I know it,' he said emphatically, knocking his pipe against the side of the chair. 'Jarvis didn't do it himself, but he put somebody up to it.'

I couldn't understand why this respectable-looking scrap dealer should want to write 'THIS IS YOUR LAST CHANCE' on the side of somebody else's greenhouse, and then come round to offer his sympathies. I was confused, and I said as much.

'Everybody's got to trust somebody at some time,' said Tom, quietly as we got back to work with the paint stripper.

I didn't say anything, trying to catch his meaning.

'Are you to be trusted?' he continued.

I blinked at him from behind my glasses.

'I think so,' I said.

'I reckon you are,' he went on. 'Ever told any lies, apart from that little yarn you spun me yesterday about looking for a job?'

'Yes, a few.' I said, the guilt I had felt yesterday returning.

I told him about the trouble at school and Hovis, and the curiosity and the need for somewhere safe and warm to go which had brought me to the glasshouse. I told him how I had been nearly killed by the train, and I tried to explain to him the kind of impression the glasshouse had made on me when I first saw it.

When I'd finished, he looked at me long and hard with his ancient eyes and said, 'Things were more straight-forward when I was a boy. We all knew what was right and what was wrong. Everything's changed now. I'm glad I've not got my time again. I've worked hard all my life, and taken nothing from nobody. That's the way it should be, and it's been a good life. Yes, you seem to be honest all right; a rare enough quality these days. Sometimes I think the likes of you and I are . . . well, you know, we're nearly extinct!'

As we worked on he told me more about the eccentric Mrs Philpot.

At one time she had owned all the land as far as the main road. What was now the scrapyard had been an orchard. In the early 1960s she found that the cost of running her father's house was beyond her means. She needed money for repairs, and so she had no alternative but to sell off the orchard.

The highest bidder had been old Mr Jarvis, the scrap merchant's father. Like his son, he was a plausible man. He told Mrs Philpot that he was planning to build a retirement bungalow for himself and his wife. The orchard was ideal because it was large enough for the house, and there would be enough land left over to stable his granddaughter's pony.

This part of his story appealed to the childless Mrs Philpot, who hoped to watch the young girl from her bedroom window, atop a Shetland pony, trotting merrily around the orchard in the summer sunshine. Alice Philpot would then be in sight of the daughter she'd never had.

The bungalow was never built. Old Mr Jarvis moved down to Torquay with his wife. There was never any granddaughter. The young Mr Jarvis was a bachelor, and moved a caravan into the orchard. The caravan became his office. Corrugated tin fencing went up around the orchard, the trees came down one day when a bulldozer appeared on the site, and scrap metal started to pile up among the daisies. It had been like that ever since.

Mrs Philpot withdrew further into herself and her glasshouse.

'That's terrible!' I said at last. 'Didn't anyone try to stop him?'

'No,' said Tom, with that same pitying look in his eye. 'Nobody cares about that kind of thing. Anyroad, the Jarvis clan have always been in cahoots with the council.'

'Well, what's all this got to do with this message on the glass?' I asked, beginning to see that things were more complicated than I ever imagined. I wasn't the only one with problems.

'This?' said Tom, scrubbing at the glass. 'This means Jarvis wants us out. He wants the rest of the garden. He thought he was on to a winner when Mrs Philpot took ill and had to go into a home. No one wants to buy a big house like this in this sort of position, with a scrapyard on one side and the railway line on the other. People who could afford it want to live somewhere with a decent view and a bit of peace and quiet.'

'Well, why doesn't he just buy it from her then? That seems simple enough to me.'

'But that's the snag. Mrs Philpot won't sell. She'll never sell, not until she's completed her project. She can't sell the house without selling the glasshouse. Anyway, after what happened last time, she doesn't trust anyone except me.'

By this time we were on to the last of Jarvis's words. Tom sat down whilst I finished off.

'Why's Jarvis getting at you then? You can't make up Mrs Philpot's mind for her. You can't make her sell. You just work here.'

'Jarvis is cleverer than that. He's worked out that the glasshouse is important. Without me, there'd be no one to take the thing on, and then he thinks Mrs Philpot will have to sell to him. He reckons he can get rid of me, and then offer Mrs Philpot more money than anybody else. What he's too stupid to realize is that Mrs Philpot loathes him so much she'd do anything to keep the land from him, even if I was to go and the project was to fail. She knows he's up to no good.'

'Is he?' I asked.

'He's up to no good with me, that's for sure. And as for his business, I don't know whether he's straight or not. The rumour is that he wants to move out of the scrap business and become a property tycoon! That's why he wants the garden. Taken with the old orchard it's just right for putting up small factory units. What with business booming in this part of the world, he stands to make a whole packet of money. He's already offered me inducements to leave, as he puts it.'

Jarvis had offered to get Tom a better council house in one of the villages round about, and a couple of thousand quid. Tom wouldn't budge. He held his old-fashioned loyalties dear, and said that at his time of life some things were more important than others. Taking bribes was low on his list of priorities.

The message on the window was the first stage in a campaign of intimidation. We certainly had something in common.

*

As we sat with our tea, feeling righteous and proud of our labours, and full of wild ideas for resisting the menaces of Jarvis and his henchmen, I put a proposition to Tom.

'Look,' I said. 'I don't know what this project of Mrs Philpot's is, and I don't want to ask, but it's obviously important. If Jarvis is out to ruin it, then things are going to get a bit difficult. I mean, you can't be here twenty-four hours a day.'

I stopped, hesitant about suggesting the next bit. I seemed to be having the wrong effect. Tom was beginning to look forlorn. He couldn't cope with the burden of the glasshouse alone and he knew it.

'Why don't you let me help you guard the glasshouse?' I said cheerfully, as though it was the easiest thing in the world.

Tom didn't react in the way I had hoped. He didn't say anything, but stared thoughtfully into his empty mug.

'Well,' I continued, 'you know I get booted out of the house every evening. How about if I came down here, instead of wandering round the streets? I could keep a look out, maybe rig up an alarm or something?'

Tom wasn't sure.

'I don't know,' he said. 'Jarvis isn't a very nice character.'

'Look at it this way,' I said. 'I need somewhere to keep warm, and you need an alarm system. If things got difficult, I could always run away down the railway line. Anyway, if this Jarvis is so clever, he's not going to hurt a kid. I don't think that would go down very well with his mates on the council, would it?'

Tom was wavering. He stared at the banana plant as if seeking reassurance.

'Why not give it a try?' I urged. 'You needn't tell Mrs Philpot.'

At long last Tom made up his mind.

'Thanks for the offer. It's best not to look a gift horse in the mouth. We'll give it a try.' But then he added ominously, 'What happens when you have to go back to bed?'

I hadn't really thought that one out, but I was beginning to get a few ideas.

'Just leave that to me,' I said, sounding rather more confident than I was in reality. 'We can work something out. I'll start tonight. If you stay till just after six, I'll come and take over.'

'You mean start tonight?' said Tom, surprised by the speed at which events were moving.

'Why not? Sooner the better,' I said.

'In that case, then,' said Tom, beginning to smile again, 'I'd better tell you about Mrs Philpot's project. After all, if you are going to be a part of it, then at the very least I owe you an explanation.'

And it was the explanation which took up the rest of the morning.

After Sunday lunch, I had to take Ginny down to the rec. Her chattering and constant demands took my mind off things as we idled on the swings, but at tea-time I began to get butterflies in my stomach. All sorts of fears crept into my imagination, and I began to wonder what I had let myself in for. I'd found a way into the warm glow of the glasshouse, but I certainly hadn't anticipated all that it entailed.

For the first time in my life I was going to be entrusted with a grown-up job. Looking after Ginny was one thing, but looking after the glasshouse at night was another. I was scared. I got the runs and had to leave the tea table twice. For one awful moment my mum started to insist that if I was off colour I should stay in. For once, Jeff's temper was on my side. As he grew impatient with my visits to the toilet, his anger began to boil. My mother saw the danger signs and dropped her insistence that I remain in the warm.

At quarter past six, I left the house. I cut down the railway line and met Tom in the glasshouse. Tom wasn't anxious to leave me alone. He'd been having some second thoughts. He was coughing too much for my liking though, and I insisted he went home, arguing that his missus would worry about him if he didn't turn up for his tea. He looked worn out.

When he'd gone, I sat on Tom's smoking chair in the dark, with my feet on an old wooden beer crate. The moon cast a silver light across the rows of plants as I settled down to wait.

The glasshouse had a life of its own. The heating pipes hummed softly and the fans breathed on and off; the whole structure creaked. I became like the soul of a man whose bones had turned brittle; I was deep within him as he settled down to rest.

As the wind gusted, the glass rattled. Then there were periods of intense silence when you could have heard a beetle scuttling across the floor or a mouse skirting the wall outside. The wind played tricks; shadows scurried across the glass. The moon came and went quickly, reappeared suddenly and then was blotted out again, as if the night were full of holes. The glasshouse floated in the uncharted and unfathomable darkness.

Attacks threatened from the trains' noisy shadows. Nothing happened. Eerie aromas were mixed into a narcotic cocktail by the fans. In the absence of Tom's pipe the glasshouse was less cosy, and took on a ghostly aspect. The glass itself offered no protection from attack. I woke with a start as I ducked the talons of a mechanical owl which came crashing noiseless through the roof on whispering metal wings. The glasshouse was in silence. The moon was gone. I had no sense of how much time had passed. Then the fans clicked on. I was rooted to the chair. My knuckles were terrifyingly white. Carlos, now just a plain banana plant, seemed a stranger to me. Where I expected a reassuring movement beyond the plants, there was none. I stared, and then minute by minute the plants seemed to grow taller all around me. It was a trick of the mind, but I raced to the glasshouse door, fumbled with the lock, fled to the fence, and scrambled up the railway embankment in terror.

Lying in bed, I felt ashamed. I had to do better, but I made no attempt to return to the glasshouse that night.

Chapter 9

Following the terror of the previous night, I had to face the new horror of catching the school bus with my mother. I pleaded with her to get a later one, but she had made the appointment with the school for nine-fifteen. I was to be readmitted at the earliest opportunity.

The journey was a nightmare. We were forced to travel upstairs because the lower deck was full, and as we tried to find a seat all the kids stared at me. I had to sit wedged up against the window next to my mum for the whole journey, listening to comments which I knew were about me but I couldn't hear clearly. I heard odd snippets and words every now and then, and they weren't pleasant. My mother kept her eyes grimly forward. I think she was trying not to listen.

My mother was the only adult on the top deck, but her presence didn't make a blind bit of difference to the behaviour. Everyone was smoking and swearing.

Just as we turned into School Road, and the nightmare was about to end, a partially consumed fish-paste sandwich landed in my mum's lap, squirting margarine all over her best skirt. She didn't know what to do. She was angry, but intimidated. She half turned round in her seat, then changed her mind and didn't say anything. There was a lot of laughter coming from the back. It was the most humiliating bus journey of my life.

When the bus eventually stopped everybody piled off, and we were left sitting alone on the top deck. Neither of us could think of a thing to say. I was ashamed of myself, my mum and everybody else.

I let my mum get off first, and walked into school a few paces behind her, grimly trying to disown her. The place was as depressing as before. It hadn't changed while I'd been away.

We were early, and had to wait outside Mustapha's office. Eventually he appeared round the corner, coming from the VIP bog with his greasy coffee percolator.

He disappeared into his office without saying a word.

My mother sat on one of the chairs beneath the notice board by Crease's door, and I stood next to her.

There were a few dog-eared lists stapled loosely to the notice board. They flapped around every time one of the doors in the corridor was opened or shut. The remainder of the board was covered in obscene graffiti, and at the bottom was a crude cartoon of Crease doing something unmentionable to a sheep. I averted my eyes quickly, but they kept being drawn back to it. The picture was horribly fascinating. I wondered how anyone had the nerve to draw it, and whether Crease had noticed it yet.

At nine-thirty we were still there. Smoke was again curling from the gap under Mustapha's door. My mother looked impatiently at her watch, but wasn't prepared to assert herself. I was in no hurry either.

At a quarter to ten Crease turned up, a little out of breath, carrying a manila file. It was mine.

'Good morning, Mrs Harding, hasn't Mr Bottomly seen you yet?' he said, looking a little embarrassed.

My mother shook her head shyly. I wished she'd speak up.

'My mum's Mrs Smith,' I told Crease.

'Oh, I am sorry, Mrs Smith,' he apologized. 'I'll just see if Mr Bottomly's ready for you.'

As Crease disappeared into Mustapha's office, I could hear the rustling of a newspaper, and through the half-open door I saw a pair of feet slide off the desk. A coffee mug fell on to the floor with a crash.

'Shit!' was the only word I heard before the door was slammed shut.

My mother and I exchanged glances, and for the first time since leaving home she smiled.

'Right funny lot here, aren't they, Wayne?'

'Certainly are!' I replied.

Then the door opened and Crease came out.

'Mrs Smith. Wayne, you too. Would you come this way, please?'

Mustapha's office was about the size of a large walk-in cupboard, like the one the caretaker used for his coffee break, the main difference being that this office had a grimy window, partially obscured by a dusty venetian blind which fanned out limply from the top left-hand corner, like a broken wing.

The sun shone in brightly, picking out the dust and the sticky coffee rings on Mustapha's desk. Mustapha's newspaper had been hastily stuffed into a black bin liner which straggled over the back of his chair.

Mustapha fumbled around with an untidy heap of papers on his desk until his trembling fingers had pushed them into some semblance of order. He was a real scruff-bag. His suit was crumpled as though he'd slept in it. Specks of dandruff stippled his untidy beard. He was the kind of man who left his briefcase at home and took ill before important meetings. His few classes always worked on paper, and more often than not he'd conveniently lose their feeble efforts, so he wouldn't have to spend time marking them.

Mustapha was totally shambolic. A few faded Christmas

cards still clung to his office wall, decaying slowly like dead moths.

Crease had arranged chairs for us beside the window, which meant Mustapha had to blink blindly into the sun through his bloodshot eyes.

My mother and I sat down, and Crease took a seat beside us. Mustapha made a hesitant beginning. My mother composed herself, and carefully covered the greasy stain on her skirt with her coat. She seemed to be more at ease now that she realized what Mustapha was really like.

Mustapha rummaged through his jacket pockets before locating what he wanted. He pulled out a stubby cigar butt and relit it.

'Now let me see, Mrs Smith,' he said, exhaling a plume of blue smoke. 'Wayne, here, was excluded for writing a threatening message about Mr Johnson, the Head of Modern Languages, on the girls' toilet wall and . . . er . . . trying to flush all his books down the lavatory. This is a very serious matter . . .'

At this point in his bumbling speech, someone let rip a real silent-but-deadly nostril-crippler of a fart. It certainly wasn't me! And from the way my mum and Crease began to gag, I knew the s.b.d. could only have been produced by Mustapha the Magnificent himself.

Farts have an unfortunate effect on me. They make me giggle uncontrollably. This fabulous specimen was no different. I felt I was going to explode. My shoulders began to shake, and I rattled like an old bedstead. My mother started too. Crease stared intently at my file, as if examining my medical record for some reference to a chronic and ultimately terminal bowel disorder. Then his shoulders began to vibrate as well. Mustapha reddened beneath his beard, but droned on, until my mother interrupted.

'Excuse me, Mr Bottomly, do you mind if I open the window? The smell of your cigar is ... a ... a little overpowering and the fumes will be bad for Wayne's asthma.'

I could have died. But at the same time I felt proud of her for having the guts to say something at last.

There was an uncomfortable pause while Crease struggled with the window. Then Mustapha resumed. I bit my bottom lip, and pulled myself together.

I didn't take much notice of what was being said, but it boiled down to my return to school being allowed on the condition that I behaved myself in future. I had to sign a sheet of paper saying that I promised to be a good boy. My mum signed it too, without a protest.

We all shook hands and said our goodbyes.

When we were safely out of the office and back in the fresh air, my mum said, 'I hope that wasn't you, Wayne, who made that nasty smell in there?' She gave me one of her rare hugs.

'No,' I said as she let me go, 'that was Mustapha Crap.'

'Who?' she shouted, looking appalled, but I was already across the yard and on my way to my first lesson.

History was half-way over when I got there. A supply teacher was in charge, if that's what you could call it. A pair of compasses winged past me and stuck into the notice board as I entered the room.

Half the class seemed to be running round the room with more energy than they would ever dream of displaying in the gym, and the rest were sat at their desks chatting.

The poor supply teacher was probably a harassed housewife with two kids screaming at home, who'd forgotten what teaching was really like. She was cowering behind her desk, pretending to be engrossed in marking.

Nappy was away with his back again. Nappy was okay, a little old-fashioned in his ways perhaps, but at least he could control us. Nappy Potter had been teaching for years.

'I was teaching when you lot were still in nappies,' he'd remind us at frequent intervals, and thus he had acquired his name, but he was held in awe and was regarded with affection. Like Rimbold, another member of the original staff, he was looking for early retirement.

Sharla was sitting at a table on her own in the middle of the room. I shoved my way over and sat down next to her.

'Hello, Wayne,' she said, smiling. 'Welcome back! You're just in time to catch the end of another really brilliant lesson. Bet you're glad you made it in time!'

I suddenly felt nervous, and the butterflies started up again in my stomach. I thought she looked gorgeous.

'Where's Becca?' I asked.

'Period pains,' she replied matter-of-factly.

I blushed every time Sharla used this phrase. I should have been used to it by now, because Becca had more periods than anyone else in the history of the universe. Her all-time record was three in one month. No one at school had twigged yet.

'You mean she's skiving again?' I said.

'Shh! Not so loud. No, she's actually got them this time, believe it or not.'

I turned a paler shade of beetroot again.

Sharla changed the subject, and asked me how I'd got on downstairs with Mustapha and Crease.

I was just beginning to tell her when Mr Bellamy, the Head of Humanities, burst into the room. You didn't mess about with him. The whole room went quiet. The supply teacher began to get to her feet, but changed her mind half-way and sat down looking embarrassed. I thought she was going to cry.

Mr Bellamy had dragged Wilkes in behind him. He dangled from Mr Bellamy's hand like a rabbit. We waited for the eruption. There was a ripple of expectant conversation. Wilkes was a poser, and most of us were looking forward to him getting it.

Mr Bellamy ignored the supply teacher completely and flung Wilkes into the front row of desks.

'Sit down, lad!' he screamed. Wilkes clawed his way into a seat. 'This idiot has just climbed out of the window! Not once, not twice, but three times during the course of this lesson. Looking for bananas, were you, Wilkes? It's a pity we're not on the third floor.'

He paused to let the effect of his words sink into Wilkes's slow brain, and to let us savour the moment of Wilkes's humiliation. Then he went on:

'I will not have this kind of barbaric behaviour in this school. You are here to learn, not to fool about. I want to see you all with your heads down before I leave the room, and you won't utter a word until the end of the lesson. I shall be next door. Wilkes! You will come with me.'

Wilkes got out of his seat and began to follow Mr Bellamy from the room. He'd been drinking cider on the school bus again and couldn't resist one last swaggering gesture. Wilkes turned and flicked two fingers up at the supply teacher. Mr Bellamy chose that moment to swivel round. He clouted Wilkes hard on the head with the back of his hand and sent him sprawling in front of the blackboard, and that was how Wilkes got suspended!

At lunch-time, Mr Bellamy made the mistake of parking his car behind the supermarket. All four tyres were slashed. No one saw it. No one could prove anything. But everyone knew the truth of the matter, including Mr Bellamy. I didn't fancy Wilkes's chances after that.

There were two good things about school that day. One was that, because Becca was away, I spent every break-time with Sharla. The other was Hovis's absence from school, and this was a particular bonus in view of the threatening note he had shoved through my door.

Sharla was the easiest person in the world to talk to. She never interrupted what you were saying with some completely different line of conversation. She listened to everything as if it was the most important thing she'd heard all day.

At lunch-time we sat on the path behind the music room, and I told her the truth about jumping out of the window, and moaned a lot about Hovis, while the choir sang raucously in the background.

At last, she patted my arm and said, 'I think it's about time you did something about him, Wayne.'

'Like what?' I said, sounding none too hopeful.

'Dunno, stick up to him. He might leave you alone then.'

'That's what everybody says,' I groaned.

'Are you saying I'm like everybody else?' she replied indignantly.

I'd hurt her feelings, so I tried to make up for it.

'No! I didn't mean that. What I meant was, he's twice the size of me. I couldn't hope to beat him.'

Sharla sank into deep thought. The Junior Choir lapsed into silence, and there was an almighty scraping of chairs in the music room signalling the end of practice. The bell for afternoon school was about to go.

We got up and walked reluctantly back towards the main block. Half-way across the yard Sharla stopped and caught my arm.

'I didn't say you had to fight him head on, did I? Haven't you learned anything in school?'

'Don't think so,' I said. 'Have you?'

'Not much. Well, not much you're supposed to. What I meant was, we've done the Second World War, right?'

We'd done the Second World War in under two weeks, like the Americans do Europe.

'Yes,' I said, wondering what that had to do with anything.

'And we did the French Resistance, right?'

'So?' I said, still puzzled.

'God, you're thick sometimes, Wayne!' she shouted, thumping me hard on the arm. With a punch like that, perhaps she'd volunteer to fight Hovis for me.

'I can't help it,' I said, pushing her on towards the entrance to the building.

Sharla continued her obscure line of thought as we pushed our way into the main block through a crowd of brawling sprogs.

'Now listen, dimbo. Hovis is the Germans and you are the French Resistance, right? Get it? Or do you want me to explain it again very slowly?'

'No, it's all right, Sharla. I get it, but how do I do it?'

'I dunno,' she said cheerfully, as though she'd just solved all my problems, which was funny, because I was sure they were only beginning. 'You've got half a brain somewhere inside that gogglehead of yours. You'll think of something. I'll try to think of something as well. One and a half brains is better than none, so you ought to feel sorry for Hovis.'

It took me a while to work that one out, and by the time I did, Sharla was mingling with the other kids in the form room and I didn't see her again after that. She stuck close to the other girls and studiously ignored me all afternoon.

*

There was one bad thing about school that day, apart from the tedium of lessons. There was a message from Rimbold demanding to know why I hadn't turned up for the football-lace practice he'd promised me. I had to see him first thing next day to explain myself.

I had forgotten to go. It seemed to me that suspension was punishment enough for all those things I hadn't done, but now it looked like I'd be in for a double dose of Rimbold's own brand of torture.

Jeff's car was parked outside Patel's when I came round the corner on my way home from school. He looked none too happy when he stepped out of the shop and saw me walking past. He had a porno magazine in his hand, rolled up in a tube, so only the cigarette advert on the back showed. I wondered what my mum would think about that.

We stood awkwardly in the street, not quite knowing what to say.

'Had a good day?' I asked.

'Not bad,' he said in a distracted sort of way and went round the other side of the car to open the door. He chucked the magazine on the back seat, no longer making a pretence of hiding it.

I tried to keep him engaged in conversation a little longer. I'd seen Hovis out of the corner of my eye, coming out of Patel's.

'See you on Monday,' his note had said.

'Where've you been today, Jeff?' I asked.

'Yeovil,' he replied. He wasn't keen to say more. 'I've got to go out. I'll see you later.'

He flashed a glance back towards the doorway of Patel's, and with that climbed into the car and started the engine.

Before he pulled away from the kerb, I shot across the road to the safety of home. I looked back as I went round the side of the house. Hovis was standing on the pavement outside Patel's, watching Jeff's car disappear down the road.

Chapter 10

I was very wary and more than a little nervous as I set off to the glasshouse that evening, in case Hovis was still hanging about. Instead of following the roads to the level crossing, I cut across back gardens, and when there was no alternative to crossing the street I did so in the darkest places. Televisions were on in every house, and my unorthodox progress passed unnoticed. If Hovis was in the area, then I'd outwitted him.

Tom was pleased to see me. I had intended letting him believe I'd spent the whole of the previous night in the glasshouse, but when I saw the trusting grin on his face I had to own up to the awful truth that I'd been scared witless and fled.

'You done the best you can,' he said kindly. 'I can't say I'd fancy spending all night here in the dark on my own. Anyway no harm's done. I guess Jarvis will wait to see what effect he's had on me before he tries again. I think he might leave us alone for a short while.'

Tom put the kettle on, and stared at me gravely.

'Look, I want to talk to you. I'm going to see Mrs Philpot tomorrow afternoon. I've been giving it some thought. I think we ought to play it straight. I ought to tell her about you.'

He paused.

'What do you think, Wayne?'

This was an unexpected turn of events. My immediate reaction was one of selfish panic. What if she prohibited me from coming to the glasshouse? I couldn't bear the thought of having this wonderful place snatched from me so soon after being granted admission to it.

'I don't know. I've never thought about it,' I said.

'Yes you have,' Tom said. 'I can see what's going through your mind. I don't reckon it'll come to that. Mrs Philpot cares a lot about her project, and she trusts me. I don't think I should betray that trust by covering up, do you? Would that be right?'

'No,' I said glumly.

'You trust me?' he said.

'Yes,' I said at last, knowing that Tom was right, but still not particularly happy about it.

'Good lad!' he said, patting my knee.

Then Tom started to root around under the staging. When he emerged, he was holding a thin book and a pencil light.

'I've got to go in a minute. I thought this might help you understand what's going on here. You need to understand some things about the project.'

He handed me the book and the light.

The book was old and beautifully bound in soft red leather. The print was sharp and crisp, and there were many meticulous illustrations. It was called *An Introduction to Orchids* by R. A. Fletcher. I stared at it in amazement.

'Yes, it was written by Mrs Philpot's father,' said Tom, in answer to the question forming on my lips. 'Read it all. It'll take your mind off your troubles . . . Oh, and if things get too much for you here again, don't worry, just go home. I think we'll be all right for a bit.'

'No, I think I'll be okay this time,' I said, determined to face up to the night ahead. It would be no different from being there by day; it would just be dark, that was all. At least that's what I tried to tell myself.

'Well, look after yourself, and have a good read. You'd best use the torch and not keep the lights on. I'll see you tomorrow, then.'

'Bye,' I said, as he made his way to the door.

The lights went off and the door rasped shut.

When Tom had gone I turned my attention to the book, and because it was written by Mrs Philpot's father it had a special interest for me which might not have been there otherwise. I hoped it would help me understand the project, because when Tom first told me about it, I had been disappointed. To my mind the whole idea was bizarre and rather uninteresting.

When Tom had explained things, I still didn't understand much, and I got the impression that Tom, despite his green fingers, was beginning to struggle a little himself. Mrs Philpot had set her heart on perfecting a new hybrid orchid, the most exotic flower, to be named after her late husband, Billy Philpot, the humble farm worker. This was her project and her obsession. Tom said she'd been working on it for years, and was not far from achieving success when she had fallen ill. It was a painstaking process which needed years of patience, trying to produce just the right combination of colours. I found the object of her passion baffling at first, but I could at least admire her persistence and dedication. It saddened me that she couldn't stay well long enough to see it through. I felt a strong tie of loyalty to her and Tom, because of what they had given me. Really I only became interested in the project, because it was so much part and parcel of them.

I had never seen an orchid in flower before Tom gave me that book. Tom had described them to me, but there were none blooming in the glasshouse at that time of year to show me. Cunningly, Tom had held the book back until now. The way a clever angler would do it, he had been winding me in, slowly but surely, like a very hungry fish on lightweight line.

Yesterday Tom had shown me the orchid plants he was nurturing in the glasshouse. They were green and somewhat spiky. They reminded me of daffodils just after they'd flowered, except there were long brown bits at the bottom of each leaf. I couldn't see what all the fuss was about until I opened the book.

The pictures were delicate watercolours, of the kind that art teachers could only dream about. The paintings more than matched Tom's attempts at describing the beauty of the flowers. The blooms were full of light and appeared to stick out tongues of fire provocatively from each page.

The book described how some of the flowers were seven inches across. They were exotic and magical, from a wilder world than the quiet of English country gardens.

These were the blooms which had become Alice Philpot's passion; an attempt to recreate the spirit and energy of her youth, and the lost love which had disappeared with it. That was how Tom had described it to me. It sounded a little far-fetched to me, I thought, but it was a romantic gesture of the kind I was beginning to understand with my new feelings about Sharla. Even so, while Sharla was bright and sunny in the same way as you might describe a dandelion, orchids were something else.

Mrs Philpot's father went on and on about them in the book, and it became obvious that orchids were popular, but how something that difficult to grow, let alone get to produce new varieties, could be popular was beyond me. It gave me a headache just to think about it, and yet I couldn't put the book down. Perhaps it was reading by torchlight which gave me the headache, or it may have been the thought of all that passion and perfume. Once you've glimpsed one of those flowers, the image is impossible to forget.

Eventually I set the book down gently on the bench, and let it rest amongst the clutter Tom always left. I paced up and down between the staging lost in thought, absent-mindedly playing a thin beam of light over the racks of plants. The glasshouse was full of orchids. They were dormant now and waiting on their new growth, but in the autumn they would burst suddenly into bloom, a last flourish of colour as the lengthening nights began to draw the winter in. Now it was all dullness and drabness, all hidden potential, a power waiting silently to be released. The heating pipes rumbled with hot water and the fans breathed on and off.

The responsibility for all this now lay on Tom. Without him, all those years of work would amount to nothing. It would all disappear as if it had never been. Only the dust in the pots would remain.

'Marrows and carrots is one thing,' he'd said as we sipped hot sweet tea, 'but orchids, well, that's another.' And then he'd added, 'But it's never too late to learn. Besides, its Mrs Philpot's passion and her project, so who are we to argue?'

He'd quickly got into the habit of talking about 'we' and 'us'. As far as he was concerned, I was now part of the glasshouse and the AP project. And it was true, the glasshouse and the project were rapidly becoming part of me.

Alice Philpot's burning ambition was to propagate a bloom with five petals of sunset pink, the perfect pink, and a tongue-like lip of poppy red, streaked with yellow flame. She was nearly there, if only Tom and I could follow her instructions and keep the glasshouse warm and safe, and if only she could live that long.

As I sat down once again to continue reading by torchlight in this improbable setting, the words of Alice Philpot's father skated across the surface of my mind. My real thoughts were now on Sharla and what she had said to me that afternoon. For once I felt goofy only on the outside; inside I was strong, and I needed to be as I began to plan my revenge on Hovis and Jeff.

Half an hour after returning home to be banged up for the night, I eased open my bedroom window with the intention of slipping back to the glasshouse and staying the night.

A waste pipe ran at an angle from the bathroom, next door to my room, and passed beneath my windowsill before joining the downpipe which also served the house next door. This downpipe marked the boundary between the two properties.

I climbed on to the sill and backed out of the window so my knees rested on the ledge. For a few seconds I clung on to the frame, calming myself, telling myself not to look down. Then I took a deep breath and let my right leg dangle, before feeling around for a foothold on the pipe. This was easier than I expected.

'So far so good.'

I spoke to myself under my breath to buoy my confidence up.

I tested the pipe to see if it would support my weight.

It felt firm enough. I wedged my foot against a join in the pipe so I wouldn't slip.

The wind blew up under my jacket and blustered round the house. I couldn't hear anything from indoors. Anyway there was no going back, so I eased the other foot down on to the pipe, and closed the window as best I could, fixing it on the last hole on the catch, so it wouldn't bang back and forth in the night.

The windowsill was dry, and I was able to hold on to it as I worked my way down the slope of the pipe. The most dangerous moment arrived when I ran out of sill to hold on to and I had to make a lunge for the downpipe.

Only practice could make perfect, but as I had never climbed down before, all I had to rely on was luck; judgement had nothing to do with it. I pushed against the wall, and at the same time let myself topple awkwardly sideways until my hands could scrabble at the pipe. Once I got a hold, I pressed my cheek against its cold metal and hung on until my breathing settled down. Only then did I dare to shuffle my feet along the pipe that supported them.

I made a mess of descending the downpipe. It should have been the easiest section to negotiate, but I lost my grip, as my knee gave way, and slid down the last five feet, grazing my face painfully on the wall. After all the tension, this was the last straw and I felt like sitting on the ground and crying. It was only the vulnerability of my position in the garden that made me get up and continue on my way.

I crept round the house stealthily, but once through the gate I clattered off down the road, and only slowed down when I got to Patel's Mini-Market, round the corner from our house.

'In a hurry aren't you, Twiggs? I thought it was past your bedtime'.

Hovis stepped out of the doorway. There was somebody else in there with him, but I didn't stop to find out who the girl was. I fled towards the main road, and put some distance between us before he started after me. Fear is a great motivator and I managed an extra burst of speed. I wanted to lead him somewhere public, where he daren't attack me, so I headed for the main road. Where I would go after that I wasn't sure. That was all academic anyway, because Hovis caught up with me where the main road was at its narrowest and the pavement was almost non-existent.

He tripped me from behind and I crashed down into the gutter. As suddenly as I had fallen, I found myself being hauled up by my collar; a car roared past.

'Next time I won't bother picking you up,' he said, breathing beer and fags in my face. 'In fact, next time I'll just kick you under an artic! That is, if you don't do what I say.'

I got the distinct impression from looking at his furious features that he was going to knee me in the face, but instead he twisted me round and tapped my head lightly against the wall of the house immediately behind us.

'What do you want?' I said, feeling dizzy. I was angry with myself for being powerless to do anything. Cars roared past, but nobody stopped. The rest of humanity was indoors watching TV. Meanwhile, Hovis was threatening to spread my brains all over their doorsteps.

It was difficult to hear much of what Hovis said above the noise of the traffic; the pain in my head confused me so I couldn't concentrate. His words seemed to be coming from a different world.

He was talking to me about the shed. Hovis wanted something from our shed, which was presumably why he had left me that note, but I still couldn't understand what there could be in our shed that he would want. Then in a lull in the traffic, I got the message loud and clear. He wanted whatever it was that Jeff kept under the floor-boards. Hovis kept on about a package, and he wanted it tomorrow.

'I know it's there,' he said. 'I've been watching. I've heard him hammering. You'd better get it for me if you know what's good for you.'

'I'll tell Jeff,' I said desperately, praying for an early release.

'No you won't!' screamed Hovis, swinging me back into the gutter.

Did he mean I wouldn't because I loathed Jeff so much, or because I wouldn't dare for fear of what Hovis would do to me if I did? I couldn't make it out.

'Bring it to me tomorrow,' he hissed and dragged me back on to the pavement. He was flinging me about like a turkey with a broken neck.

'Not possible!' I shouted as the traffic noise rose to yet another crescendo.

'Why not?' he screamed in reply, turning me around so I was facing the road again. As the bus passed he jerked me towards it, only pulling me back from the brink of annihilation at the last possible moment. I yelled out, and he put his hand over my mouth to gag me. It was a disgusting, greasy hand, and it smelt of chips.

But then, as suddenly as this horror had begun, it ended. Hovis dropped me, and all at once was running back up the road in the direction from which he had chased me.

I looked up from where he'd left me sprawling on the pavement and saw a spinning blue light reflected distantly in the window of the car showroom opposite.

The light, and then the noise came nearer. Only an ambulance. But it was enough to have saved me from Hovis. It sailed past me as I raced up the road towards the scrapyard.

I ran down the alleyway and clawed desperately at the door in the garden wall. It was unlocked, and it shouldn't have been.

There was someone in the garden. As I came round the side of the house I could see a torch beam playing over the surface of the glasshouse. Then there was a tinkle of glass and the torch seemed to go out.

I was as mad as hell, and hurt by Hovis. I didn't care any more. Someone was attacking the one thing which had come to mean something to me. I ran down the garden, yelling like a hysterical child, and fell headlong over the wheelbarrow, which Tom had left beside the path.

When I came to my senses, someone was standing over me. A chill ran down my spine. Like a hedgehog I tried to curl up into a ball and hide my face, but the torch never wavered from my head.

'What are you doing here?' The voice was thin and rasping.

Then the question was repeated: 'What are you doing here?'

I didn't say anything.

'Sit up, boy! If you persist in lying there like a slug among the cabbages, I'll have to take my shoe and beat the living daylights out of you.'

There was no arguing with a command like that. I sat up. Still I couldn't see the face behind the torch.

'What are you doing here?' came the question again. 'Answer me, or you'll be answering to the police.'

'Tom asked me to come,' was the best that I could muster. My knee was killing me again.

'Tom who?' the voice persisted. The torch was unwavering in its hold on my face.

'You know, Tom. Tom who works here.'

There was a pause in our strained conversation as a train went past. The torch then moved away from my face and began to pick out a path towards the glasshouse.

'You'd better come with me and tell me about it,' said the voice, still fierce in the darkness. I was compelled to follow the steps of a small shadowy figure. The alternative was to go back to the estate and face Hovis.

The torch stopped at the glasshouse, and then turned its attention back on me.

'Are you old enough to be out this late?' the voice asked, a shade more kindly, in the manner of an old-fashioned schoolma'am who had begun to regret her earlier hasty words.

'I'm fifteen,' I said meekly.

'I see. And what's your name?'

'Wayne,' I said.

'And you say you are a friend of Tom's?'

'Yes,' I said, wishing my interrogator would move the blinding torch away from my face.

'Well then, as you're here, Wayne, and seemingly invited, albeit unofficially, welcome to my glasshouse!'

So the voice, hovering in the dark, belonged to Alice Philpot!

'I'm afraid I've made a bit of a mess of this pane of glass here. Tom will be cross. Clumsy me, I dropped the torch when I was looking for my key.'

'Look, perhaps it would help if I unlocked the door with my key,' I suggested, and immediately knew that I had landed Tom right in it.

'Oh, I see,' said Mrs Philpot meaningfully. 'I see . . . Well, I suppose I did leave him in charge, foolhardy though that may have been.'

'Look,' I said, 'I didn't mean to get Tom into trouble . . .'

'No, no, I can see you didn't.'

The torch beam still played relentlessly on my face; all this while the old lady had been scrutinizing me from the safety of the dark.

'Mrs Philpot,' I suggested, 'could you shine the torch on the lock for a minute? Then perhaps I could open the door.'

'Yes, yes,' she said, 'let's get in out of the cold for a moment. You can help me look around. It's not that I don't trust Tom, but he hasn't had as much experience with these things as I have, and I do like to be sure.'

It was a relief to find the torch pointed somewhere else for a change. I unlocked the door and we went in. Mrs Philpot switched the light on and for the first time I could see her clearly. She was not the wild, romantic figure Tom had painted, nor was she the exotic bloom which had filled my imagination. It was as hard for me to think of her as ever having been passionately and obsessively in love as it was to imagine that the withered-looking plants surrounding us in their pots of crusty peat could splash out again in a heady and dizzying display of colour fit to set the humid air of the glasshouse humming.

Mrs Philpot was a small, wizened old lady with bright, grey eyes. Her stroke had taken away the use of one arm, but other than that she was all there. She had all her marbles, and her lively mind clattered from subject to subject like a pinball machine. Her passion, outwardly at least, had turned to enthusiasm, but she betrayed nothing of what she still felt inside for Billy Philpot, who'd died so young, so long ago.

As we sat round the kettle, she told me of her escape from the nursing home, dramatizing it with flamboyant gestures from her good hand. She hated their rules and regulations. The nurses wouldn't let her come back to her house, but she was determined. Once she'd set her mind on checking the glasshouse, nothing was going to stand in her way. A lot of questions followed. What was I doing here at this time of night, she wanted to know, and what on earth had I done to my face? Why were my glasses chipped, and what was my mother thinking of, letting me get so skinny?

I told her as much as I could, leaving out the bit about

Mr Jarvis. That was up to Tom to tell her. I explained that Tom was going to see her tomorrow, to let her know all about me.

Mrs Philpot was visibly relieved that Tom and I had decided to work together, and her face settled into an easier, more relaxed kind of weariness. She had been concerned that Tom wouldn't be able to cope on his own, and was particularly worried about the safety of the glasshouse at night. It had been preying on her mind.

As the time came for Mrs Philpot to go, she took one last tour of her plants. Then I escorted her back to the main road, where she had arranged to meet the taxi which had brought her from the nursing home.

Before the taxi drove off, she wound the window down and said, 'I don't know when I'll be able to escape again. It's all so very tiring.'

'I know,' I said.

In the yellow light of the street lamp, Mrs Philpot didn't look very well.

'I can rest more easily now,' she said. 'I hope I'll see you again soon.'

'Don't worry,' I assured her, but I felt none too confident. 'We'll look after the project!'

'Give my love to Carlos,' she said cheerily, and summoning the last of her energy, wound up the window.

I watched the taxi disappear round the bend in the road, and then I returned to the glasshouse. Mrs Philpot had entrusted me with the key to the garden door.

I found a piece of board and some tape, and made a temporary repair to the glasshouse, where the torch had fallen through. Then, before settling down to sleep on the blankets he had left for me, I wrote Tom a note to explain what had happened and to tell him that everything was squared with Mrs Philpot. When I'd finished, I taped it to the staging next to the kettle, and settled down into the blankets on the floor.

Events whirled round in my head, and then stopped. The glasshouse hummed softly; the fans clicked on and off. The tropical night inside the glasshouse breathed all around me, and I wasn't scared any more.

But I was dog-tired, and soon fell asleep.

Chapter 11

I woke with a start as the glasshouse door opened. Sunlight was streaming in through the roof. I was too drugged with sleep to move. For a moment I felt disorientated and couldn't understand what was going on. All I could see was sacks of shredded bark stacked under the staging.

'Anyone at home?'

It was Tom's voice. He was early.

'Morning everybody!' he called cheerfully to the plants.

I rolled over and blinked in the direction of the door. Tom was walking towards me.

'Wayne!' he cried. 'Are you still here?'

I raised myself on to one elbow; I ached all over.

'You're early, Tom,' I said. 'What time is it?'

'Half past eight,' he replied. 'Shouldn't you be somewhere else?'

'Half eight!' I screamed, jumping out from under the blankets so fast that my head spun, and I had to sit down again.

'It can't be,' I groaned. 'Oh, no!'

I sat on the floor with my head in my hands.

'What am I going to do? I should be on my way to school, and I've missed my paper round. I haven't even got my school uniform on!'

It was Tom who decided what to do next. He simply took over. He didn't think it was a good idea to miss school. As far as he was concerned, work was a virtue and he held education in the highest respect. Tom also wanted to keep me from getting into further trouble, so soon after my suspension.

'Ever been on a motorbike?' he said.

The full implication of what he said took a few moments to sink in. He wanted me to get on the back of his bike. I was frightened of motorbikes, and the thought of getting on behind someone who might drop down dead at any moment wasn't very appealing. That sounds a bit cruel, but that was how I felt.

'No,' I said in answer to his question, hoping that he wouldn't pursue the matter.

'Never too soon to learn,' he chuckled cheerfully, like a small boy up to a prank. I didn't really want to move at all; my mouth felt like the inside of a vacuum cleaner.

'First stop, the paper shop. You can have the missus's helmet. Come on, we haven't got all day.'

There was no alternative; I followed with hardly a protest.

As we locked up the glasshouse, I felt like a man being led to the gallows.

'Don't look so glum,' he said. 'It'll be fun. But we'll have to be quick if we're to get there in time.'

His last words were the ones I'd been dreading.

'Look, it doesn't matter if we're a few minutes late,' I said, hoping for a last-minute reprieve.

Tom didn't hear. He'd already disappeared round the back of the glasshouse to fetch his Triumph.

'Put this on,' he said as we wheeled the bike up to the track outside the house. 'It's not very glamorous, but it'll do.'

The helmet looked like a peeled orange which had been rolled round in the dirt a few times, or more chillingly, like a ball of grubby bandages hiding a severed head.

Tom wedged it over my skull. It nearly tore my ears off,

being such a tight fit. Then he yanked the strap under my chin, so hard my teeth banged together.

'Right, climb on!' Tom shouted. 'Just remember, hang on to the strap behind me, and lean over when I lean over. That way we won't fall off.'

This hardly filled me with confidence.

'How old is this thing?' I shouted into his ear, as I groped for the seat strap.

'Thirty years,' he replied. 'I've had it from new. Only thing wrong with it is the springs in the saddle have gone. Got to ride it a bit like a horse!'

I didn't dare ask the age of the tyres. They were as bald as Tom, and not much younger by the look of them.

'Hang on!' he shouted, and kicked the bike into life. It was a bloodthirsty beast. It shot forward, spitting gravel from the back wheels. I was bucked backwards and forwards as we took off, and roared, zig-zagging, down the alley. Tom braked hard at the main road, then flung the bike hard left. Before I could get a firm grip, we were leaping along the main road itself.

Tom screeched to a halt at Frocesters' where I did my paper round, and rushed inside. He was out again in a flash, and we were bound for my house. There Tom jettisoned me at the door.

'You get changed, and I'll circle the block,' he said as I tried to regain my balance on the pavement. 'Be quick, and don't take that helmet off. There's no time.'

I hurtled up the path, unlocked the front door and took the stairs three at a time.

My mum was out, taking Ginny to school. The explanations would have to wait until later. If you ever want to feel stupid, try changing your clothes while wearing a crash helmet. Standing in front of the mirror, I looked like an albino Mekon.

Before leaving, I scribbled my mum a hasty note about the papers being late. I grabbed a Mars Bar from the cupboard, and left the house as quickly as I'd arrived.

Tom was already revving the bike next to the kerb. We had seven minutes in which to get to school.

'We'll really have to get a move on now,' Tom shouted gleefully above the throb of the engine. 'I'll have to open her right up!'

Down by Patel's we flew past my mother on her way home. She didn't notice us. Tom, ever mindful of children and stray dogs, took the estate at a steady fifty miles an hour.

The main road was jammed with traffic which had tailed back for two miles from the roundabout near school. Tom gunned the old Triumph hard at the junction, and we leapt across the road to join the stream of cars. Tom didn't believe in queuing. He swung the bike out wildly and we roared down the white line in the centre of the road. I could hardly bear to look. Tom pushed the bike faster and faster until we were going flat out. A bus loomed up in front of us like a train about to burst out of a cinema screen. Tom hit the brakes and swung the bike into the gap left by a considerate post office van. The bus flashed its lights blindingly, and its horn screamed as it rumbled past. Instantly, Tom swung the bike out again into the middle of the road, and the next thing I knew we were heaving into the roundabout at speed. I leaned over hard, my knees nearly touching the ground, and I thought I was going to be flung off. I shut my eyes. When I opened them again we were tearing down the last stretch of straight road, before turning off into the street which led to school.

By the time we roared into the school yard, I was a quivering wreck.

'A minute to spare,' said Tom. 'I've not driven like that

for years. There's life in the old dog yet! How's your bum, son?'

My backside was the last thing on my mind at that precise moment. I was overjoyed to be alive and absolutely motionless.

'Oh, fine,' I said casually. 'Thanks for the lift.'

My hands were shaking so much I couldn't get my helmet off.

'Here, let me,' said Tom, whose fingers were as sure as the day he'd learned to ride.

By now a group of hungry sprogs had gathered around us. For once they were speechless.

'So, you fancy one of these then do you, Wayne?' asked Tom, patting his bike.

'Oh yeah, some day when I can afford it,' I said.

I hoped that day wouldn't come for a very long time.

Then the bell went, and Tom shot off to do my paper round, waving as he rode off down School Road like the Lone Ranger's long-lost grandad. There hadn't even been time to tell him about Mrs Philpot.

'Who was that?' said Sharla, coming up behind me.

'Pierre of the Resistance, ma petite!' I said, pushing her in the direction of school.

The day got off to a good start. When I went to see Rimbold he was surprisingly pleasant. It was obvious that something good had happened to him overnight. Perhaps he'd made the big sports-equipment deal he was always talking about. I imagined he even dreamed about training shoes, stacked in bright boxes from floor to ceiling.

Rimbold was doing pull-ups from the central-heating pipes, which ran across the ceiling of the changing rooms. He asked me if I wanted a try at it, but I politely declined, saying I didn't really feel up to it at the moment. Then he somersaulted down from the pipe and made me an offer on some training shoes at rock-bottom prices. I didn't quite know what to say.

'No, you're not really the sporty type are you, Wayne?'

'No, more like the spotty type, really,' I said, speaking from the heart.

Rimbold actually laughed at that. It was the first time he'd laughed at anything I'd said; normally it was the things I did that he found funny.

'Look,' he went on, 'I reckon you've had it a bit rough recently, and therefore I'm prepared to forget the football-lace treatment if you tidy up the equipment cage at lunch-time. How's that sound?'

'Brilliant,' I said, overcome by the realization that Rimbold wasn't so bad after all. 'It's a deal!'

I held out my hand to shake his.

'Don't get too cocky, son,' he said, making out he was going to shake my hand, but at the last minute his own hand whipped up and clipped me behind the ear. Then, by way of a final warning as I pushed through the changing-room doors, he kicked me hard up the bum like a kid taking a swing at a coke can.

Becca was still away, and I found myself beginning to nestle closer and closer to Sharla in English. It was Valentine's Day. A lot of kids in the class were looking at cards. Sharla didn't seem to have any. I began to wish I'd bought her one. She didn't seem to notice me nestling up to her, but went right on with the Mills and Boon she was reading.

English was a fairly civilized lesson. Our teacher, Mrs Roebuck, was a bit of a character. Her husband was an actor on television who specialized in playing intergalactic bus drivers on sci-fi series and villains in sleazy cop programmes. Mrs Roebuck was eccentric, and would stop us in the middle of a piece of work to read a poem she'd come across while flicking through an anthology at her desk. She was one of those loud women who are always losing hair-grips and have stray strands sticking out all over the place from their makeshift hair-dos. Mrs Roebuck was rarely still, and did everything in a rush.

We didn't do much in Mrs Roebuck's lesson, except Sharla of course, who read and read as much romantic fiction as she could lay her hands on, but at least we didn't muck about. Mrs Roebuck specialized in personal writing. She would keep on telling us how much she valued what we had to say. I'm not quite sure what she was on about, but she was a kind-hearted old biddy who meant well.

Mrs Roebuck's husband was our school's main claim to fame. Apart from John Roebuck, we were notorious for producing swell-head amateur footballers, the occasional Page 3 girl, and petty criminals. The school didn't add up to much, but leaving aside Hovis and his gang, it was usually okay, that is if you ignored the majority of teachers, which most of us did.

I was quite comfortable in English, supposedly working on my piece about our Ginny, but spending most of my time looking out of the window and doodling pictures of winged warriors in the margins of my exercise book; such a small scale these flying figures looked more like fairies. When I wasn't doing this I was trying to snuggle up to Sharla.

I could see Hovis two floors below me. He took a subject we all called Skiving Skills, which was what all the kids who didn't do exams, or who the teachers couldn't control, had to do. Mustapha was in charge of this Life Skills group and he couldn't control them either.

It was car-washing day today. Hovis and his mates had

gone round threatening the staff to let them wash their cars. If they didn't, then there would be real trouble. They charged fifty pence, and the money was meant for the new mini-bus fund, which was a bit rich, because it was the Life Skills kids who'd destroyed the old one. Raising money was a slow business, and we could only guess where the money really went.

Hovis was in the yard with a couple of kids I didn't know, a pair of right drongos by the look of it. They stood around admiring Hovis as if he was some famous work of art. Hovis was leaning against the wing of Johnson's kit-car, a little two-seater with a tatty spoiler on the back which looked like it had been added as an afterthought. It was the sort of car which would have been more at home in a Scalextric set. The doors were open and the radio was blaring. Hovis stood there like a wally, pretending it was his.

Eventually they started to clean it, a process which lasted ten minutes and consisted of throwing buckets of water at it. Johnson wasn't going to be very pleased, because although they'd shut the doors, they'd left the windows open, and the radio had become ominously silent.

They soon got bored with their work, and started fooling about. Hovis spent the last ten minutes of the lesson throwing buckets of water up in the air and trying to run away before the whole lot came down again. By the time the bell went the gormless idiot was soaked, and his two mates were beside themselves at the ingenuity and talent of their friend.

Meanwhile, from my position on the second floor, I felt as safe as houses, and began to develop an idea for fixing the pathetic Hovis. Watching him behaving like a five-year-old, it was hard to imagine that this was the same kid who nearly pushed me under a bus on the evening before, and was threatening worse to come if I didn't get him whatever was inside the shed.

Sharla was right about the best form of resistance and Rimbold was right about getting too cocky. Tom was right about trust, and up there on the second floor it felt good to know that for the first time in my life I had friends. I had Tom and Mrs Philpot, I was beginning to win Sharla round and I had the glasshouse.

All the same, the pathetic Hovis was still dangerous. I could only afford to tangle with him if it was on my terms.

At break-time Hovis was getting it in the ear from Johnson for soaking the inside of his car, and I took the opportunity to make the rounds amongst the sprogs, in search of balloons. Sprogs always had all sorts of odd things in their pockets and pencilcases, most of it nicked from the news-agent's on the way to school. I knew the sprogs quite well, and generally they did what they were told.

When I first asked about balloons there was a lot of giggling and falling about. Eventually, I got some sense out of them and was told I ought to see Jimmy James, a big spotty kid in the second year, because he'd got some.

I found Jimmy James bouncing up and down on the fence by the allotments. I didn't know him too well. He was nearly as tall as me. A crowd of excited sprogs had gathered around him, and he was enjoying his audience.

I shoved my way through the crush, and said, 'I heard you've got some balloons. Can you let me have some?'

He nearly choked, and laughed so much he fell off the fence and rolled about among the cabbages. All the sprogs jumped up and down like a bunch of monkeys fighting over a banana.

When the smartarse recovered himself, he said, 'Stuff me, even Wayne Harding's at it!'

Then there was more mirth all round. I felt so small, I was nearly swallowed up by my shoes, and I wished I'd hidden in the Resources Centre as usual.

'The balloons.' He pronounced the word in such a way as to let everybody know I was being left out of some private joke. 'The balloons will cost yer,' he continued, 'if you really want them.'

He chewed noisily on his gum while he waited for my answer. He was growing up to be like Hovis.

I hadn't anticipated all this trouble, but I had to go through with it or I'd look more of an idiot than I already was. There was no way I could bully him into handing them over, like I could a sprog.

'How much?' I said.

'50p,' he said, trying to play the hard man. 'They're really good-quality balloons!'

I felt in my pockets and counted out the coins. I had 39p and a lot of fluff.

'I've got 39p and that's all,' I said. 'It's 39p or nothing.'

It seemed like a lot of money to pay for a few balloons, but I'd made up my mind about Hovis, and it all seemed to boil down to a question of supply and demand. I couldn't afford any more time to look further afield. I had to get Hovis before he got me.

Jimmy James remained silent for a moment, eyeing me scornfully, enjoying the power he had over me. I tried not to look too eager, or anxious.

At last he said, 'Okay!' and slapped my hand in phoney American style.

I handed over the money, and the sprogs held their breath, savouring every moment of the transaction. Jimmy James gave me the glossy packet.

'These aren't . . .' I began to say, but stopped as I realized what he'd given me.

'Have a good time!' he shouted, so everybody in the vicinity could hear. The sprogs burst into life again and screamed at me until my ears burned.

'Oh yeah,' I said, unable to think of anything more witty to get me off the hook. I blushed and blundered off through the crowd.

One of the sprogs caught up with me near the building.

'You should have asked me,' he said. 'I'd have given you them for 20p. Wilkes was selling them outside the school gate this morning for 15p. All the Fourth Years have got them!'

I had to act quickly, because at second break Hovis would be looking for me, and as it happened the condoms proved to be far better than balloons. In fact they were just the job.

During Home Economics I told Sharla about my plan. At first she was horrified, but when she realized there would be no danger for her, and that only Hovis would get it, she came round and began to get quite excited about it. My original intention had been to use greasy washing-up water, but it was Sharla's wicked imagination which came up with the devastating effects of custard.

Mrs Fowler, our Home Ec. teacher, was easily diverted. She loved to get involved in pally conversation with us. Mrs Fowler thought she was wonderful and understood kids. She imagined she was one of us and that we thought of her as our friend. We just laughed at her behind her back. She wore the most hideous suits with brightly coloured tights. She had a big bum, and today she was wearing a stripey number which was about as subtle as a circus tent.

Sharla engaged her in a conversation about colour co-ordination at the other end of the room, while I swiped a pint of milk from the fridge and some custard powder from the cupboard.

The custard was cooling nicely in a plastic measuring jug by the time Sharla came back. It was all ready.

As we sat round waiting for our quiche to cook I told Sharla about the package under the shed, and Hovis's attempt to beat me up on the main road. Then we wrote the note:

DEAR HOVIS

    MEET ME IN THE RED CANYON AT BREAK.
    I'VE GOT WHAT YOU WANT.

We didn't sign it, just in case it got picked up somewhere later. I didn't want anything to incriminate me.

When the custard had cooled, I asked Mrs Fowler if I could go to the bog.

'Of course you can, Wayne,' she said in that sugary way of hers. 'You're one of the few boys I can trust.'

Little did she know.

Sharla diverted her attention again while I stuffed the jug of custard into my carrier bag and left the room. I ducked into the girls' bog for safety, and locked myself in a cubicle.

What followed was quite messy. I'd never actually handled a condom before, though I'd seen them lying about the yard from time to time and hanging from the hedges along the cross-country course.

I definitely didn't like the oily feel of this one, and the custard which spilled on to my hand made it worse. It took me about ten minutes to pour the pint of custard into the condom. I lost a bit down the bog, but not much.

By the time I'd finished, the condom bomb was very sticky and difficult to handle, so I dangled it down the pan and pulled the chain. That removed most of the excess custard.

I placed the bomb carefully in the carrier bag, and

carried it gingerly out of the toilets. It was so heavy and wobbly that I felt it was bound to burst before I reached the top landing on the staircase above the Canyon. The custard trembled obscenely inside the bag as I supported the weight of it with my hand.

My heart pounded as I climbed the stairs, but inside the classroom either side of each landing lessons continued undisturbed. I placed the bag conspicuously on top of the fire extinguisher at the head of the staircase. Kids were always leaving rubbish there. No one would bother investigating it, and no one would take responsibility for clearing it away. It was perfectly safe.

The whole operation took fifteen minutes, and when I returned to the lesson, Mrs Fowler wanted to know where I'd been. I said I'd been sick, and like the idiot she was she sent me to the Medical Room, giving me the freedom to do exactly what I wanted. Sharla promised to clear up my cooking for me at break-time.

Instead of going to the Medical Room, I went straight back to the Canyon, and took up my position on the second landing. Ten minutes before the bell for break, I saw Sharla cross the yard as planned with the message for Hovis; she'd told Mrs Fowler her period had just started. Hovis was in the Computer Room, and there wasn't much chance of Crease actually being there teaching him.

A few minutes later, I saw Sharla going back to her lesson. She did not look up as she crossed the yard, but returned to Mrs Fowler looking as innocent as the day she was born.

From the landing above the Canyon I had a clear view of the path Hovis would have to take. I myself had an escape route. The doors off the landing led into classrooms, which in the old block were arranged back to back with a connecting door. The doors were kept open during the day because of fire regulations. All I had to do was let loose the custard condom and beat a retreat through the classrooms and down the next staircase to the Resources Centre, which was always teeming with kids at break-time. I'd be gone from the landing before anyone realized what had happened.

The instant the bell went, two classes came rushing on to the landing, teachers in their midst hot-footing it to the staffroom for coffee. No one took the slightest bit of notice of me.

As the day was warm and bright for the time of year, most of the kids streamed outside, leaving only a residue of diehards loitering in the Canyon below. Hovis would soon get rid of them.

I kept watch through the big plate-glass window, careful to stay out of sight in the alcove immediately outside the classroom.

It wasn't very long before I saw Hovis crossing the yard. He appeared to be eager and excited. I could see that he was trying hard to act normal, but instead of shoving kids out of his way as he strutted across the yard, he sidestepped them.

I took out the condom bomb, and balanced it carefully in my hand. Its capacity was phenomenal. I could have squeezed three pints in if there'd been time.

When Hovis disappeared from my sight, I eased the custard condom on to the banister. I peered down into the Canyon.

Where was he? There was a commotion going on, with a lot of shoving and pushing and shouting. A door slammed hard, and someone screamed. Hovis was clearing the Canyon.

I couldn't bear the suspense much longer. My hands

sweated and I began to lose a proper grip on the bulging condom.

Then for a split second Hovis appeared in the stair-well below.

I let the condom bomb loose. It fell smoothly and fast, with satisfying obedience to the law of gravity. It appeared to get smaller very quickly. Then there was a dull, soggy splat as it hit Hovis on the left ear and burst all over the place like a huge pustular boil.

At that point, I grabbed the carrier bag, ran into the classroom behind me and shot through the dividing door like Charlie Chaplin late for a train.

By the time I got on to the next staircase I was gasping for breath. I couldn't believe I'd done it. On the next landing kids were climbing over each other to get a view out of the window. More kids were tumbling out of the Resources Centre.

In the yard below there was uproar. A crowd had gathered round Hovis, who was thoroughly smeared in custard, and then a cheer went up as Crease emerged in a similar state, because I must have got him too as he came into the Canyon to investigate the disturbance Hovis had caused. There would be hell to pay, if I ever got caught.

The window on the landing began to bend and bulge under the pounding of feet and fists, and as the crowd in the yard hooted and whistled with Hovis and Crease trapped in their midst like defeated prize-fighters, the huge pane of glass finally cracked. At this moment, in fear of disaster on the landing, and out of terror for my own discovery, I punched the fire alarm and released the pent-up energy of the school in the jubilant pan-demonium of fire practice.

*

Out on the tennis courts where we lined up in form groups to be counted by our tutors, Sharla drew me to one side and whispered in my ear, 'Did you do this too, Wayne?'

'Yeah, had to,' I said. 'The window on the staircase was about to break, and apart from that, it seemed like a good way of escaping. No one will be able to remember where I was now. I'll just say I was in the medical room. Fowler won't have checked.'

'It's a pity I missed Crease and Hovis. I'd have loved to have seen Crease. Everybody's talking about it. They all reckon it was Wilkes sneaking back in.'

'Suits me if it stays that way!' I said.

'Well, I never thought you had it in you, Wayne,' she said as we began to move back towards school. Break was not going to be extended because of the fire alarm. Mustapha wanted to get things back to normal as soon as possible.

'I didn't think I could do it either,' I said, feeling proud of myself. 'Don't tell anyone, will you?'

'Me! What do you take me for?'

'Sorry,' I said as we swept with the mob through the door of New Block.

There was a big buzz going round the school, and it was humming in Computer Studies. Crease didn't appear, and the rumour was he'd taken Hovis home and then gone off himself. It seemed likely that neither of them would be back for the rest of the day.

Sure enough, they stayed away. As far as Hovis was concerned, that had been my intention, but I was a bit miffed I'd been the cause of getting Crease half a day off. It didn't please his classes either, because covering teachers tended to stay in the room. Still, you can't have it all ways.

At lunch-time Sharla phoned her dad at the sorting

office and asked if he'd come and pick us up after school because she was worried about Hovis getting me on the way home. Sharla was convinced that he would know who'd humiliated him. I didn't see how he could, it seemed just about everyone had condoms in school that day, and Hovis was too dumb to think I'd have the nerve to pull a stunt like that. All the same, I wasn't going to complain about getting a lift home with Sharla.

I was there when she phoned her dad. She was dead straight with him and told him I was in trouble, but much to my relief left out the part about the condom, the custard and the fire bell. She was lucky having a dad like that.

At lunch-time I tidied the equipment cage for Rimbold, and in the afternoon I managed to survive games by thinking about being in the car with Sharla. I kept warm by dodging around trying to avoid contact with the ball.

When the lift eventually came, Sharla sat in the front, and I sat on my own in the back. I was disappointed, and then felt ashamed for being so ungrateful.

As we left school safely behind us my disappointment turned to relief. You couldn't have everything and, despite my problems, I was beginning to think that I had more going for me than most.

Sharla's dad dropped me at the door, and after that day at school even home seemed a relief.

Chapter 12

When I got in, there was another package for Jeff on the hall table. It was the same type of Jiffy bag, but this time it had a Bournemouth postmark. It had been franked at a place called Hamlyn Hobbyists, and was stamped with the cheerful message: 'FUN FOR ALL THE FAMILY SINCE 1902'. Perhaps it was something for Ginny's birthday. It couldn't possibly be what Hovis was after.

I still couldn't understand why Jeff should hide anything under the shed, unless he kept his pile of dirty magazines there so that my mum wouldn't find them. Instead of reading the paper in the shed after tea, perhaps he read dirty books. It wouldn't have surprised me in the least if Hovis wanted that sort of thing.

It still didn't add up though, because Hovis could get magazines anywhere, unless these were particularly unsavoury, the sort you couldn't buy in shops. Apart from that, what was his connection with Jeff?

The two packages I'd seen seemed innocent enough. It was quite likely, as I'd first thought, that they were not what Hovis wanted at all. It was something else which Jeff was hiding. The whole thing was confusing, and a total mystery to me. It was impossible to get into the shed before Jeff came home, so I'd have to bide my time, and in the meantime avoid Hovis.

At half past six I followed my safe route across the back gardens and returned to the glasshouse via the railway line.

Tom was full of smiles and still basking in the glory of the morning's bike ride. He'd also enjoyed doing my paper round, and was contemplating getting one of his own. He had already put himself down on the waiting list at Patel's.

Tom thanked me for my note about Mrs Philpot, and began to tell me the details of his visit to see her. After the excitement of the night before, Mrs Philpot had taken to her bed again.

'I cheered her up though,' said Tom, as if to say he was still God's gift to women.

'Oh? How?' I inquired.

'Well, we hatched a plan.'

Conspiracies seemed to be the order of the day.

'I'll tell you about it,' he said, rubbing his hands together, 'while we get the kettle on.'

Tom was stringing me along and enjoying every minute of it.

'Come on, Tom,' I said, 'tell me now!'

'Oh, all right then, if I must ...' He paused dramatically and lit his pipe. 'Mrs Philpot's going to sell the house to Jarvis.'

I was dumbstruck.

'No! She can't! I don't believe it!'

'True,' he said. 'We decided it was for the best under the circumstances.'

'You're joking! What about Billy Philpot's orchid, Flaming June, or whatever she's going to call it?'

Tom broke into a broad grin and patted my knee.

'Convincing aren't I? You've got to admit I had you going there!'

'What?' I said. 'You mean, she's not going to sell it?'

'Shh! Not so loud,' he whispered confidentially. 'Jarvis might hear. You never know. A few weeds in here might be on his side. They could take over if he got hold of the place!'

'Come on, Tom,' I said. 'Stop messing about. What's going on?'

I couldn't stand much more of his fooling around.

'Well, it's like this. I'm going to let Jarvis know that Mrs Philpot's decided to sell, but only she, you and I know she's not going to. So don't let on.'

'I wouldn't dream of it,' I said. 'But what's the point of all this pretending?'

'Let me explain,' he said, putting down his pipe. 'But not until we've got the kettle on.'

There was no way round him this time. I'd have to wait.

'How was your day, anyway?' he asked, changing the subject as we shuffled the mugs around on the staging. 'Hectic as getting there?'

'Sort of,' I said noncommitally. Two could play his game.

'Well, come on then. Out with it!'

Tom was all ears like a conspiratorial schoolboy.

I drew a deep breath.

'Come on, come on, don't keep me in suspense!' he said.

'I got Hovis with a custard condom ... and Mr Crease!'

'What? What are you talking about?'

Tom was completely bemused.

'I'll tell you when you've told me why you're going to let Jarvis think Mrs Philpot is going to sell.'

Tom knew he'd lost this round, so he told me more about his plan while he finished making the coffee.

'Simple,' he said. 'Two reasons. Reason Number One: if Jarvis thinks he's buying the land, he won't cause any more trouble. That buys us time. Buying and selling property can take a very long time, particularly when you're dealing with dotty old ladies who take ill and become incoherent at crucial stages of the negotiations, if you get my meaning. We reckon we can string Jarvis along, at least until the orchids have bloomed.'

'I hope it works,' I said, still feeling slightly uneasy about the idea. 'What's the other reason for doing it, then?'

'Ah, this is the really nice bit. Solicitors cost money. Mrs Philpot's won't have to do much, but Jarvis's will. We'll wait and wait, and then we'll pull out of the deal at the last minute. The house will no longer be for sale. Jarvis will be left with a hefty solicitor's bill to pay, and nothing to show for it. Serve him right!'

Tom slapped his knee loudly, and refilled his pipe.

It all sounded too easy. Something was bound to go wrong.

'But what happens when you pull out? Won't Jarvis be hopping mad?'

'Course he will,' said Tom, 'but we'll have thought of something else by then.'

He didn't sound too sure about this last bit. We finished our coffee in silence, lost in our thoughts.

Then it was my turn to tell my story. Tom chuckled and slapped the bench at intervals, particularly when the action hotted up. He roared with laughter until his eyes streamed when I came to the bit about Crease getting covered in custard, and winked at me meaningfully whenever I mentioned Sharla.

During all this it occurred to me that I no longer had to guard the glasshouse. For a while it could slip back from centre stage. Tom was going round to see Jarvis later that night; he'd already phoned to arrange the meeting. The glasshouse would still be my home base, but one of my burdens had been lifted from me.

When Tom had gone, I gave the subject of Hovis some more thought. I had won a minor victory at school, and the custard attack gave me great satisfaction, but I had by no means concluded the war with Hovis. Hovis would be shocked for a while. He might even think it had been one of Jacko's pranks. They were always falling out. But if he so much as suspected it was me, then his rage and hunger for vengeance would be doubled. If he didn't suspect me, he'd still be after me to get the package from under the shed.

It was clear to me that, whichever way I looked at it, I was into a dangerous game. If I did nothing, Hovis would be out looking for me. He knew I was locked out in the evenings; everyone in the school did. Eventually he would move closer and closer to home and get wise to my back-garden trick. Sooner or later he would get me, either at school or at night.

Solving the school problem was simple. I would bunk off during the day. The other was more difficult. I was safe in the glasshouse, but if he followed me there it would offer no sanctuary. The last thing I wanted was to bring Hovis near to the orchids. Smashing the glasshouse up would be just his cup of tea.

What I decided to do had a dangerous logic. I would hunt Hovis.

I'd find him and shadow him. Then I'd pick him off when I had the opportunity. I'd be gone before he knew what had hit him. I had no idea what I'd finally do to get him off my back, but in the meantime I'd make his life very unpleasant.

At eight o'clock I locked up, and made my way along the railway. A fog had fallen, and ghostly wraiths of mist draped the sides of the embankment. On the line itself the fog was patchy and I loomed in and out of the mist. I felt strangely disembodied, like a ghost. The poor conditions slowed my progress. My ears had to be more alert, and my weak eyes more sharply focused; it was this that saved me, not from the trains, but from Hovis. He was leaning on the crossing gate, illuminated by the lights. Then the fog closed in around me. I stopped and crouched down. I listened for a moment, thinking what to do, and then, with my heart pounding, I retraced my steps along the line to the glasshouse.

There was no reason for Hovis to follow. He was expecting me to come across the tracks from up the hill, not along the line itself. Hovis had obviously followed me earlier and lost me near the railway. His mistake was that he wouldn't credit me with the guts to trespass on the main line.

His next move would be to go back to my house and lie in wait for my return at eight-thirty. I'd pick him up there and test my plan. If I tried to get into the house he'd have me. I would stay out late, and take the consequences when I eventually returned home. And I wouldn't return home until I'd done some more damage to Hovis.

I left the garden and followed the main road back towards the estate. The road was still quite clear; the fog had yet to gather.

My guess was correct. Hovis was waiting on the corner, just beyond Patel's, in a position to see both ways along the road. I ducked down out of sight behind a car which had been covered with a tarpaulin for the night.

Every now and then Hovis would look at his watch, and as time went on he checked it more frequently. He was growing impatient. I must have been crouched behind the car for a good hour before Hovis started to walk down the road towards me. My legs ached with cramp and my fingers were numb with cold, but I managed to edge round the car to keep out of sight. Hovis passed within feet of me, and by the time he'd reached the next corner, I'd worked my way along to the other end of the car. When I peered round the front wing, Hovis had disappeared.

I waited. Sure enough, Hovis appeared again. He was checking the street to see if I was going to make a dash for home.

I was presented with a new problem. Hovis was sitting astride a bike, which he must have had stashed away round the corner. He swung it round and pedalled off towards the main road.

As soon as he'd disappeared I rushed off along the pavement as fast as my gangly legs would carry me. I looked desperately down each side passage as I passed. I was nearly at the main road before I saw what I was looking for. Unfortunately it was only a kiddie's BMX, but it was better than nothing. The bike was sprawled on the front lawn. I was through the gate and pedalling away like a bandy-legged frog before I had time to reflect on the enormity of what I was doing.

At the junction, I looked left and right, and saw Hovis's back light glowing distantly through the thin veil of mist, heading in the direction of town.

The BMX had no lights, which was just as well because like a fool I'd probably have used them and been spotted straight away. As it was, I set off down the pavement. I had no hope of catching Hovis, but I could just about keep him in sight.

Hovis didn't stop for traffic lights. He was in a hurry, and just kept pedalling. A reckless show-off on a bike at the best of times, he never looked round.

I was well and truly knackered by the time I saw Hovis shove his bike into the racks outside the pedestrian precinct in the town centre, and that was where I lost sight of him. I had ducked into the door of a solicitors' for safety, and when I emerged he had gone.

The street leading up to the precinct was wide and deserted. The precinct was a concrete wasteland at night. The fountains, which brought it to life during the day, were switched off, and the combination of empty flower tubs and graffiti made it a forbidding place.

The precinct was on two levels. A concrete gallery ran round the entire area, and was linked to the lower level by concrete walkways and winding staircases. Here and there the harsh lines were broken up by illuminated hoardings, the strip lighting of which was mostly defective and flickered disturbingly like eyelids in a dream.

The precinct had been designed in the shape of a large hammer. There were three points of access. Right now Hovis could be in there somewhere or he could have left by one of the other exits.

At night this part of town was inhabited by gangs of kids who had nothing else to do. The only places open were two pubs, a chip shop and a Chinese restaurant. I'd never been into the precinct at night, and I didn't fancy it much now.

I dodged from door to door until I reached the entrance. I peered round the corner, ready to run at the first sign of Hovis heading in my direction. I needn't have worried; the precinct was empty.

Hovis's bike stood alone in the racks. It was a good bike, the kind I would have liked. The idiot had left his pump. I unclipped it and tucked it under my arm. Then I let the air out of the tyres, first the front, then the back. To make sure I'd fixed Hovis good and proper I flicked the quick-release lever on the rear wheel and worked it loose. By waggling the wheel about I tangled the chain around the derailleurs; it was a shameful waste of a chain set, but an effective way of immobilizing the bike. Then I removed the lights and went back to the doorway of the solicitors' to fit them to the BMX.

The fog had begun to cast a yellow film over the town centre as I mounted the BMX, and rode up the pavement to the precinct. I held Hovis's pump firmly across the handlebars. As I turned the corner into the precinct and pedalled fast down the slope, I kept a look-out, left and right, and cast a vigilant eye over the gallery above as well. I completed a circuit of the hammer's handle, and saw that there was no one about.

Then I parked myself back at the top of the ramp where I'd come in, and waited. There was no movement. The Chinese restaurant glowed through the mist. Tuesday night seemed poor for business.

I raced down the slope again and swung left into one side of the hammer head. A small queue huddled in the warmth of the chip shop and one or two kids were playing the machines. The pub next door was quiet. There was no sign of Hovis. At the top of the slope four kids were mucking around on a skateboard. They took no notice.

The precinct was scooped out of the earth like a bowl. Each entrance was at the top of a slope which drew people down into the shopping area, and which also made them reluctant to climb out. When it rained, the precinct became a big storm drain, and frequently flooded. Everyone complained, but nothing could be done.

The fog had thickened and settled at the bottom of the precinct where the three sections joined. I pedalled cautiously through this pool of mist and up the slope to the Brahms and Liszt, a large glass-fronted pub which was popular with under-age drinkers and young trendies. Anyone could get served in there. It was packed and the juke box was blaring.

I cycled past and left the bike at the top of the slope. After stuffing the bicycle pump up my sleeve, I walked back towards the pub.

The large windows were glazed with frosted glass etched with pictures of small orchestras, and if you looked carefully you could see that the musicians were naked. The solid window frames were stained with deep brown yacht varnish which was beginning to flake off, and here and there familiar names had been carved crudely into the woodwork. There was only one bar in the pub and the two entrances opened straight into a vast velvet lounge.

I kept watch on the Brahms and Liszt from the doorway of the television shop opposite. Each time the doors opened I tried to catch a glimpse inside. If Hovis was anywhere in the precinct, he would be here.

A hen party appeared noisily at the entrance to the precinct, shouting and singing dirty songs. They were covered in toilet paper, party poppers, strings of tinsel, and great dollops of shaving foam. Outside the pub, they stopped and pulled themselves together. Much of the toilet paper was thrown on to the pavement, and there was a great adjustment of tinsel. They groomed each other like chimpanzees after a tea party, removing what shaving foam they could. The girls giggled and flopped drunkenly against each other.

As they were about to burst into the pub I joined them, and amidst their noise and confusion I slipped in unnoticed.

The interior was lit dimly with red lamps. Compared with the cold February night, the atmosphere inside was stale and fetid. The dense smoke swirled about and stung my eyes.

I stuck close to the hen party as they moved clumsily towards the bar. The bar was heart-shaped, and was upholstered in quilted crimson leatherette. It formed an island in the centre of the room. All around the lounge were hung large mounted posters of silent movie stars. The lounge itself was subdivided into cubicles by plush velvet curtains slung from brass rails.

All the seats were taken; there was standing room only.

It was St Valentine's Massacre Night, and all drinks were half-price. The hen party was soon drawing attention to itself, so I pushed my way through the crowd and began to make a slow circuit of the room.

My small size was an advantage. I was lost in the crush. Only someone a couple of feet away would be able to see me approaching. I was completely hidden from anyone sitting down. On the other hand, obtaining a good, clear view was not easy either.

The ceiling was supported by steel pillars which stood at intervals around the room. They were faked up to look like cylindrical mirrors. The mirrors were in fact made of sheets of reflective plastic. When I spotted him, Hovis was leaning against one of these. He had his back to me, and was busy talking to someone on the other side of the pillar.

I stood stock still, or as still as I could, given that I was being jostled by the crush of drinkers. I had to fight to maintain my position, like someone treading water. Hovis was nudged aside by a girl pushing her way towards the bar. As he stepped back the person he was talking to came round the pillar. It was Jeff.

I ducked down instinctively, and barged into the bloke standing behind me, slopping his beer down his jacket. I shoved my way through the crowd double-quick and made it to the door before anyone could catch hold of me. I wrenched open the door and ran back to the bike, glad to be out in the fresh air again.

I sat on the bike feeling dazed. It was safe to return home now that I knew where Hovis was, and I'd knackered his bike. In that sense I'd done what I'd set out to do, but on the other hand I now desperately wanted to know what he was doing with Jeff. I was shocked to discover that they knew each other, and couldn't understand why they should. I could see why Hovis might drink at the Brahms and Liszt with kids his own age, but not with someone as ancient as my stepfather.

As I sat there, things began to fall into some sort of shape. Hovis and Jeff had been in Patel's at the same time. That could have been a coincidence. Hovis was interested in the cavity under the shed, which suggested that there must be some connection between the two of them. But if Hovis knew Jeff, why didn't he just ask for whatever it was he wanted? Were they friends or weren't they? Whatever they were, I didn't like the smell of it.

Then I remembered that note Hovis had shoved through our door. I'd thought it was meant for me, but was it really for Jeff?

I didn't have time to dwell on things, though. Before I could come up with any kind of answer, I saw Hovis march out of the pub and set off in the direction of the cycle racks.

He didn't see me until the last second, and then it was too late. I don't know what I must have looked like hurtling out of the fog on the BMX, swinging the bicycle pump around my head.

I shot down the slope and took him totally by surprise. The pump was fully extended, and as his stupefied face looked round, I brought it down hard on the side of his head. He stooped, clutching his ears in his hands, and collapsed in a heap. I swung the bike round fast and clouted him a second time with the pump. The top of the pump snapped off, and I brandished the jagged remains towards his face. Blood was pouring from his split scalp. Hovis was stupefied by drink and the unexpected blows, but not enough to have prevented him recognizing me. He snarled and swore angrily, but he hadn't the strength to fight back and so he staggered off in the direction of his bike, all the stuffing knocked out of him. What a day he'd had! First, to be sent home splattered in custard, and then to suffer the ultimate in humiliation . . . to be bashed about the ears with his own bicycle pump by none other than Wayne Harding, the well-known wimp and timid toe-rag!

On the ground where he'd stumbled lay a brown envelope, the sort with a window that bills come in. I picked it up and stuffed it into my jacket pocket.

I left the precinct via the chip shop entrance, and pedalled furiously back to the main road. Hovis was hurt and his bike was crippled, but he wouldn't be down for long. If he was into something with Jeff, I couldn't be sure of remaining safe in my own house, and even if Jeff didn't get me, sooner or later Hovis would come back round.

I made up my mind not to go home. I wasn't going to go to school either. There was only one safe place for me now, and that was the glasshouse.

I returned the BMX to the garden where I'd found it, leaving Hovis's bicycle lamps as interest on the loan. Then I made the eerie journey down the railway line. The glasshouse was invisible from the embankment in the dark and fog, but I reached it with the instinct of a homing pigeon.

Finally I lay down exhausted on the blankets, and considered what to do. If I'd ever needed friends, then I needed them now, because when I opened the envelope Hovis had dropped to see what was inside, I discovered that it contained £250 in used tenners.

Chapter 13

I was up and about by the time Tom arrived, and I had a pot of tea all ready for him. Tom was surprised to see me.

'No school today?' he asked like a suspicious parent.

'No,' I said. 'Not for me.'

'Like that is it?' he said, knowing from my tone of voice and the look on my face that he shouldn't push it any further. Tom was coming to understand that schools were a bit different from what they were in his day.

'I see you've got your priorities right,' he continued. 'I could murder a cup.'

'Tom,' I said, as I poured the tea, 'there's something I want to talk to you about.'

'Oh?'

'Well, a lot of things, actually.'

'Fire away,' he said jovially, taking his tea. 'Ah, that's good. Plenty in the pot?'

Tom settled into his seat.

'Want a sandwich?' he asked. 'Bacon or lamb?'

'No thanks,' I said, not wanting to deprive him of his lunch.

'Go on. I can always go home for more. The Missus always gives me loads. I think she really hopes I'll stay out for tea as well. Go on, you look starving. Have one!'

In fact I was famished, and I didn't take much persuading. I was soon tucking into the best bacon sandwich I'd ever tasted. It made me feel a lot better. The events of the night before had begun to take their toll, and I had been feeling a little light-headed ever since I woke up.

'What's been happening then?' Tom asked. 'Judging by the look of you, things must have been happening on the home front.'

'Well, it's a long story,' I said.

'I've got a long time. How about another cup of tea and a sandwich before we start?'

That seemed like a good idea.

After I'd finished my story, Tom looked grave.

'So things have got really serious then?' he said. 'In short, you don't get on with your stepdad, and Hovis is on your tail because he wants something from your stepdad, but we don't know what. Now you've attacked Hovis to try and shake him off, and because of that you can't go to school, and you can't go home either because Hovis and your stepdad might be mixed up in something together. On top of all that you've got Hovis's money, and he'll be looking to get it back. That's about it, isn't it?'

'Yes. That's about it. Not a lot really,' I said bleakly. 'What am I going to do?'

'What are *we* going to do?' said Tom cheerfully, slapping me on the shoulder. 'Don't worry, we'll sort it out.'

'Well, where do we start?' I said. 'Any ideas? My mind's gone completely blank.'

'Oh, no problem. I always reckon that in these cases the best thing to do is have another cup of tea, light up the old pipe and put your feet up for a while.'

Tom could be infuriating at times, but he had a point. There was nothing we could do right that minute.

'Why not just go to the police?' suggested Tom, sucking noisily on his pipe.

'I can't,' I said.

'Why not? If there's something fishy going on, and

there must be with all that money involved, they'll sort it out.'

'No I can't,' I repeated. 'I may hate Jeff, but I don't hate my mum. If Jeff is up to something, they may not be able to prove it, and he'll take it out on us. If they do prove it, my mum will end up with no money coming in. It's no good complaining to the police about Hovis, because I can't prove anything. There's never been any witnesses. Besides, my reputation at school isn't too high at the moment, and don't forget I hit Hovis pretty hard with that bicycle pump and knackered his bike. I could end up getting put away myself!'

I was beginning to sound quite fed up.

'Okay, okay,' said Tom. 'We just have to work all these things through so we're clear about what we can and can't do. Now, what will your mum be thinking? You didn't go home last night. She'll be out of her mind. We'll have to do something about that. Will she have gone to the police?'

'I don't know. That depends on Jeff and whether he's prepared to have the police snooping around. I suppose if he's straight he'll call them,' I said.

'Will your mum call the school?'

'No, I doubt it. Jeff hates the school and anything to do with it. No, I think they'll try to find me by themselves first. I'm not sure how much either of them really cares, when it comes down to it, but I don't want my mum worried even so.'

'Well if that's the case,' said Tom brightly, 'the first thing to do is to let her know you're all right. Next we do something about your paper round. The rest can wait.'

It was a difficult note to write. I kept starting, and then screwing it up. It was worse than anything we had to do in Mrs Roebuck's lesson. I wanted to explain things, but

157

couldn't. They sounded so incredible, and apart from that I knew that Jeff would get to read the note as well. In the end I kept it simple:

Dear Mum,

I'm all right. I'm perfectly safe. Things have been a bit difficult at home for me lately, and I need time to sort things out. I'll be back soon. Give my love to Ginny, and say hello to Jeff.

Don't worry. I'm all right.

Love,
Wayne

P.S. I've given up my paper round.

Tom agreed that this was probably the best we could do for now. The paper round was easier to deal with. Tom would drop in and say that I was ill, and wouldn't be able to do it for a couple of weeks. He'd offer to take it on in the meantime. Tom insisted we save the money and buy my mum a present with it when this was all over.

That was the other big question. When would it be all over? How long would I be away, and how would things be when I got back? Neither of us was prepared to talk about this. We avoided the issue. We made the assumption that everything would come right in the end.

Like most people we believed in happy endings.

While Tom went off to post the note through our letter box and sort out the paper round, I spent some time puzzling over the £250 Hovis had dropped.

It was more money than I'd ever had, and the only time I'd even come close to a sum that size was when Jeff gave me the fiver after his big win on the horses, if indeed that was where he'd got the money.

I tried to see things from Hovis's point of view. Even he wasn't stupid enough to go to a pub with £250 on him, so he must have been given it by Jeff. But why? And where would Jeff get it from in the first place? He didn't earn that kind of money on the removal vans. Hovis had recognized me as his attacker, and would know I'd cleared off with his envelope. He might think I was in league with Jeff in a plot to get it back, though it was just Hovis's bad luck that he'd dropped the money. None of it made much sense to me.

I had to find some answers, and the only way to do it was to keep my eye on both Hovis and Jeff. How could I do both at once? The one advantage I had was that I'd disappeared, and no one knew where I was.

Hovis would be looking for me. Jeff would pretend to look for me for my mum's sake. But right now I had the upper hand. For the time being I was as good as invisible.

When Tom returned to the glasshouse at around eleven-thirty, he was a little agitated.

'Bloody Jarvis hanging around again,' he moaned.

'What's happened?' I asked.

'Met him at the gate. He's bringing a feller to have a look round, just like he owns the place already! Says he's cleared it with Mrs Philpot's solicitor, but I doubt it. You'd better duck down out of sight under the staging until he's gone.'

I stayed there for the next half-hour, getting cramp amongst the bags of peat. Tom cleaned Carlos's leaves, and chatted away to me the whole time. Anyone outside the glasshouse seeing Tom standing in front of the banana plant and talking excitedly would think he'd finally gone off his rocker.

'That bloke drives me mad,' he muttered. 'I'll get rid of him if he comes near here. I should have put slug pellets

159

down; special big ones with five pound notes round them. That would have fixed him!'

'What are they doing?' I asked.

'Measuring up the garden,' said Tom, 'to see how little they can get away with offering for it.'

Tom gave me a running commentary on what was happening in the garden. When he slipped into a whisper I knew that Jarvis and the surveyor were coming close. He lapsed into silence as the footsteps approached. Then, suddenly, Tom shouted: 'Go on, be off with you!'

Jarvis obviously mouthed something in reply which Tom didn't like, because he rushed down the glasshouse to the door, shouting dementedly. Jarvis must have pushed off then, because Tom came back, wheezing and spluttering.

I crawled out from under the staging and sat him down. He'd gone a nasty shade of purple, and his breathing was loud and irregular. I fetched him a glass of water. His hands shook so much, his false teeth rattled against the rim of the glass.

'My missus says I shouldn't get steamed up like that. My, but I feel better afterwards,' he said when he'd recovered. 'I hate Jarvis's sort. Never done a real day's work in his life.'

'We'll fix him,' I said, passing him another glass of water. 'Come on, forget about Jarvis. Tell me what happened when you were out.'

'Ah, interesting. I went to the paper shop first, and if I say so myself, I was rather convincing. They were very sympathetic towards your . . . er . . . plight.'

'My what?' I said, beginning to feel uncomfortable.

'Your plight . . . you know . . . your illness.'

I didn't like the way he said 'illness'.

'What did you tell them?' I asked.

Tom looked a little sheepish.

'Come on!' I said. 'What have I got?'

'Piles,' he said.

'*Piles!* Why *piles?*' I shouted. 'Oh, my God!'

'I told them you couldn't sit down, see, couldn't ride the bike. I'm afraid I laid it on a bit thick.'

'You certainly did,' I said. 'I haven't got a bike! I'll never be able to go back there again. How embarrassing!'

'I got the job though,' said Tom gleefully, 'So all is not lost.'

'Yeah, I suppose not,' I said trying not to sound too gloomy. After all Tom had been out to do me a favour. I continued more brightly, 'What else happened?'

'Well, there's a lot more to tell. I got this idea at the paper shop.'

Oh my God, spare us from another bright idea, I thought, but merely said, 'Go on, what was it, Tom?'

'I was thinking about the problem of delivering the note without being seen, so I bought some envelopes, and put your mum's name and address on one.'

Hmm, really original idea, I thought, but said nothing.

'Now, here's the good bit. What I did was, I put it through the letter box of the house four doors down, by mistake on purpose, if you see what I mean. That way no one in your house could connect me with the note, not easily anyway.'

'You're a genius!' I said.

Tom's face became animated.

'There's more,' he said. 'When I drove past Patel's, there was a big lad, yobbish-looking, hanging around. You know, just pacing up and down, waiting. Looked like Hovis to me, from the way you describe him. Anyway, when I'd posted the note, I hung around to see what would happen. I did right delivering the letter to the wrong house, because your stepdad's car was still on the hard-standing. After about ten minutes, a woman came out and shoved the note through your letter box. So I hung around a little more. I sat on my bike so I could see your house and keep my eye on this other lad. I didn't have long to wait, because soon enough your front door opened, and your mum and stepdad came out with Ginny. They got in the car, and drove away. The way I see it is, they were going out to look for you.'

I was about to interrupt when Tom said, 'Wait a minute, there's still more. When they'd gone, I waited to see what that lad would do.'

Tom paused, and lit his pipe.

'What happened then?' I said, almost dying of curiosity.

'Well, this lad Hovis went over to your house, and rang the bell.'

'Do you think he thought I was in there?'

'I don't know what he thought. I dare say he'd been waiting to get you on your way to school, but he had something else to do as well, because no sooner had he finished ringing your bell than he went round the back of your house. I drove round slowly, and I could just see him down your side passage. He was doing something to the shed door. Trying to break in, it looked like. But then a neighbour of yours came out, a real old battle-axe she was, and when Hovis heard what she had to say he beat it very fast. I'm glad I don't live next door to her; I couldn't cope with that!'

'Mind you,' I said, 'nor could Hovis by the sound of it. He isn't half getting a hammering these days, what with me and now ear-bashings from old Mrs Richardson. You can understand why Mr Richardson works nights. Anyway, what did you do then?'

162

'Well, I thought about taking a look at the shed myself . . .'

'You didn't?'

'No, I decided it would be better to come straight back here. I'm no hero, what with that Mrs Richardson, and your stepdad likely to show up again.' And then Tom added ruefully, 'I'm not as quick as I used to be.'

'Not to worry,' I said, 'you did far better than I could have. Well then, what shall we do next?'

Suddenly energized, Tom replied, 'Check the plants, dampen down the floor, coke up the boiler, wash all the glass, and then . . .' He paused dramatically. 'We wait till it gets dark!'

Chapter 14

The night was bitingly cold, but more uncomfortable than the creeping numbness was the strange, ghostly feeling of spying on my own house. Tom had got a late pass from his missus, as he called it, and we were both sitting on his Triumph, outside Patel's. I wore his missus's helmet and an old pair of Tom's goggles over my specs. Tom had lent me an outside leather jerkin and, all in all, we resembled a pair of ageing kamikaze pilots, none too desperate to die. I was altered beyond recognition.

There had been no movement in the house during the past half-hour. I had a numb bum, and neither of us knew quite what we were going to do. We had a vague idea that if we followed Jeff we might learn something.

Tom was as cheerful as ever. He chuckled away to himself and every now and then he'd turn round and make dramatic fighter-pilot gestures, the meaning of which only he knew for sure.

At last the front door opened, and Jeff emerged from the house. He climbed into the car, and as he turned on the engine, Tom kicked the Triumph into life and manoeuvred it round, anticipating the direction Jeff would take.

He allowed Jeff to turn the corner towards the main road before he pulled the bike away from the kerb. We followed the car out of town towards the motorway.

Jeff stopped at the top of the slip road, and picked up a

passenger. It was too dark to make out who it was as we roared past in the dark. We joined the stream of traffic heading in the direction of Bristol, and settled into the left-hand lane.

Before long the blue Granada swept by, and Tom accelerated to keep it in sight. I held on for dear life, but the journey was not nearly as hair-raising as the ride to school and I began to enjoy it. I also began to understand the barely controllable excitement which heats the blood of the hunter.

After about ten miles Jeff pulled off the motorway into a service station. We dropped back a little and followed him cautiously up the ramp. He parked the car a long way from the main service area. We drifted into the filling station, and Tom stopped the bike out of sight, round the corner by the air lines. Jeff was some way off, but when we had dismounted we had an uninterrupted view of the car.

Jeff and his passenger remained in the car. Nothing happened for ten minutes. Then a pale blue Transit van pulled into the car park and came to a halt some twenty yards away from the Granada. Its headlights remained on for five minutes. Then they snapped off.

Jeff and his passenger got out of the car and walked towards the van. The nearside door swung open, and the two men climbed in. The van started to move, and we let it go past us before taking up pursuit on the motorbike.

At the next motorway junction the van turned off and followed the main road for about two miles before swinging hard left into a dark country lane. Each time the van slowed to take the twists and turns of the road, we slowed, keeping our distance. We lost sight of the tail-lights frequently as the lane became increasingly contorted.

165

When we emerged from one particularly long series of twists down through high banks and towering beech trees, the van was nowhere to be seen. It had disappeared, and we failed to pick it up again in the two miles which followed. Tom stopped and cut the engine.

'We've lost it,' he said, despondently.

'What happened? Do you think they saw us?' I asked.

'Yeah, well, they're bound to have noticed us. If we could see them, they could see us. Stands to reason, doesn't it?'

'Where do you think they went then?' I said, genuinely puzzled.

'Well, they could have turned off up a track, but we should have seen some sign.'

'Maybe they killed their lights and shot on ahead, and then turned off. In which case we can retrace our steps,' I said hopefully.

Tom was thoughtful.

'On the other hand, they might have pulled off to let us pass, so they could turn off later without being seen. That is, if they're up to anything at all. But all that chopping and changing and palaver on the motorway looks pretty suspicious to me.'

'What shall we do then?' I asked, hoping we could get moving again. We were stuck in the middle of nowhere and I was freezing.

'We'll pull off here,' said Tom decisively. 'We'll stay out of sight and wait. If they don't pass us in ten minutes, we'll retrace our steps, and look for a lane off.'

Reluctantly, I helped Tom push the bike on to the verge and back into the trees. Then we sat down to wait.

From far down the road a vehicle approached. It sounded wrong. A car passed, and the road became silent again.

'We'll have to go back,' I said at last, growing impatient.

'No, it's not time yet,' said Tom, listening intently. 'Do you hear that?'

There was a rustling in the branches above us, and then a rapid tapping on my helmet.

'Only the rain,' I said, as it began to tip down. 'Can't we go?'

'Shhh . . . Yes, in a minute. But listen!'

I listened, and sure enough I heard a familiar drone and rattle. Bouncing in and out of the ruts and potholes, the pale blue van swished by in a cloud of spray.

Tom started shoving the bike forward, and I pushed hard from behind. We bumped and banged it across the verge and back on to the road.

We climbed aboard and shot off through the rain. The road was incredibly dark, much darker than before. I could see the tail-lights of the van some way ahead in the inky blackness. We were riding blind, without lights.

The van was going fast in the wet, and Tom wiped his goggles furiously as we roared along, trying to keep up. Then the tail-lights disappeared suddenly. Tom braked hard and the back wheel slid away from beneath us. He released the brakes. We wobbled dangerously. Then the bike righted itself, and we shot round the nearside of the van as it pulled right into a hidden driveway, and disappeared.

'Bastards nearly killed us!' Tom shouted as he brought the bike to a skidding halt a mile further on. 'Are you all right?'

'I think so,' I said, still shaking. 'It all happened so fast. I just shut my eyes and hung on. I thought we'd had it.'

'So did I. I thought I might have dropped the bike for a moment; it's lucky I've got good tyres.'

I looked down doubtfully, and felt the tread.

'You've bought new ones,' I said.

'Yup! That race to school the other day got the old ticker going a little too fast for my liking. I thought it was about time I put some new tyres on. You know, just in case. I'm glad I did.'

'So am I,' I said, climbing off the Triumph and stretching my legs. 'What do we do now?'

'Go back, of course, and see what they're up to. We haven't come all this way for nothing.'

'Don't you reckon they'll be on the look-out for us, though?' I objected.

'No, those vans are so noisy, and they were so busy turning off, they won't have heard us.'

I wasn't so sure, but Tom was set on the idea, and as he had the transport I had no choice if I didn't want to walk home. The rain came down in rods, and I didn't really have the heart for any more adventure, but if Tom was still game, then I had to keep my end up, or else call myself chicken and give up the fight for good.

We drove slowly back along the road with the lights on, because it was now impossible to see without. Tom looked from side to side, hoping to find a decent place to stop.

We parked the bike round the bend, where it could stand unobserved by anyone walking down the drive. Tom dismounted. He looked very stiff and weary.

'Are you sure you're okay?' I inquired.

'Yes, I'll be all right in a minute; I just need to rest up for a while.'

I could see that he was going to be no practical use to anyone in this condition, so I told him, 'Give me twenty minutes. I'll go and have a look, and then come straight back.'

He began to argue.

'I'm not so sure that's a good idea,' he said. 'Perhaps we should call the whole thing off like you just said. I'm sorry I seem to have let you down at the last minute. I've just lost my puff.'

Now I was the eager one.

'Can you survive for twenty minutes?' I persisted. 'Like you said, now we're here we might as well see it through. Don't worry, I won't do anything stupid. I don't like getting hurt!'

'Well, only if you're sure,' Tom said. 'I'll get under these trees here until you come back.'

I took off the helmet and goggles, and fastened them to the bike. Tom looked a frail figure as I left him. I tramped off down the verge. I was soaked through to the skin and my trousers clung round my legs like seaweed, making the backs of my knees sore.

There was a stone wall bordering the drive where the van had turned in. I forced my way through a gap in the hedge where it adjoined the wall, and found myself in a ploughed field. I followed the wall for about thirty yards. It seemed to enclose a small estate.

Constructed of well-weathered stone as it was, the wall was fairly easy to climb, even for someone as clumsy as me. It was about eight feet high. I dropped awkwardly down the other side and saw that I was in a small copse to one side of an imposing country house.

Above me, the branches of the tangled trees clacked together and whipped about in the wind. Under cover of this noise I was able to move round to the back of the house, which was shrouded in total darkness.

As my eyes adjusted I saw that the van was parked close by with its rear doors open. A car nestled to one side of the van, but I couldn't determine what make it was.

There was movement in the house and around the van.

I crept forward to take a closer look, and lay down on the very edge of the fringe of trees. What was going on was plain to see. I didn't have to watch for long.

In my excitement and haste to get back to Tom with the news, I stood up clumsily. The headlights of the car snapped on, and for half a second, I must have appeared frozen at the edge of the beam.

I took a diagonal course through the copse, weaving in and out of the trees and leaping over roots, to get as near to the road as possible before scaling the wall and racing to the safety of Tom and his dependable Triumph.

When I reached the wall, I realized my awful mistake. Here the wall was masked by an impenetrable tangle of elder bushes. I turned and ran desperately back along it, looking for a break in the vegetation.

I had lost valuable seconds, and by the time I was straddling the top of the wall, I could see that the car had driven out on to the road and had stopped by the gap in the hedge where I had first entered the field. A pencil beam was moving steadily up the field towards me.

I clambered down the wall in a cascade of crumbling stones, and raced up the field, following the wall away from the road. All the while, the point of light was gaining on me.

Then I heard a sound, muted by the distance and my rasping breath, but recognizable as the crunch of glass, perhaps a windscreen being shattered. I looked back. The torch stopped where it was and swung round towards the road. I gained a few precious seconds, and took my opportunity, cutting left and making a dash for the middle of the field, to a point beyond the reach of the pencil beam.

A commotion arose from the road. There were raised

voices, and a lot of shouting and swearing, then the familiar sound of the Triumph's engine revving. The torch began moving along the wall. It stopped again roughly where I had turned away from the wall to cross the field. I held my breath. My luck was out. The beam began to move in my direction. Then there was another, larger, more powerful light in the field, a single thrusting beam rising and falling over the furrows. The beam was pursued by a roar and a whine as the rear wheel of the Triumph slipped and spun in the soft ground. It was Tom.

The torch stopped following me and bobbed back hastily towards the road, where the lights of the Transit van had appeared.

The Triumph stopped in the middle of the field, its engine idling, and I rushed towards it, stumbling in an ecstasy of relief. Tom was there, coughing and spattered in mud, but grinning from behind his goggles.

'Climb on!' he shouted as I approached. There was no time to put the helmet on. No sooner had my bum hit the saddle than we were bumping across the field, slithering wildly in and out of the deep ruts, until eventually we met firmer ground in the corner of the field farthest from the road. Tom gunned the bike forward, and we raced off down a footpath, leaving chaos and confusion behind.

We had no idea where we were going, except that it would be to a place safe from danger, where we couldn't be found. The footpath widened into a bridleway, and from there on the going was easy.

At the end of the bridlepath, we turned on to a lane, hoping to see a sign that would tell us where we were. It was not until we entered a neat village with a large duckpond on the green, a few miles along the road, that we could reorientate ourselves. Tom recognized it immediately as Little Ballham, famous for its brewery and Five Feathers skittles team.

Tom parked the bike outside the bus shelter, and we took cover from the wind.

'My God!' he said as we sat down. 'You all right, Wayne? We nearly didn't make it that time.'

This seemed likely to become an all-too-familiar phrase.

'What happened?' I said.

'I might well ask you the same thing, young man. Back in twenty minutes, you said. You seemed to have stirred up half the county!'

I told Tom my side of the story, and how I'd bodged it at the last minute. Then Tom told me about his end of it.

Never being one to sit down for long, Tom had decided to take an amble along the verge. Ditches were interesting places, he said, and you never knew what you might find. So he had set off with the intention of keeping warm, and passing the time by looking for pieces of junk which might come in handy one day.

'I was just having a poke about, see,' he said, 'when I heard that car start up, and the way it raced down the drive, I reckoned something must be happening. I was still a bit away from the bike when that first chap with the torch got out, so I took a grip on this old bit of exhaust pipe I was having a look at. I couldn't do much from where I was, but I thought I could at least try to immobilize the car, so I got a good hold on the old exhaust pipe and hurled it at the windscreen. That seemed just the job. I hadn't realized there was still somebody sat inside. That accounts for all the screaming you heard. Then I ran back to the bike, and you know the rest. God, my missus will fair murder me when she sees the state I'm in. She'll kill me good and proper!'

I couldn't imagine anyone trying to murder Tom and succeeding. He'd tried hard enough to kill himself on more than one occasion since I'd met him, and he'd failed miserably each time.

'What a night!' I said. 'Still, we know what Jeff's up to now. Well, sort of, anyway.'

'But we still don't know where Hovis fits into all this do we?'

'No, but sooner or later, we'll find out,' I replied, cheerfully.

'Shall we call the cops?'

I wasn't sure whether Tom was serious, or just testing the water.

'No,' I replied, 'not until we've nailed Hovis.'

'In that case then,' said Tom, getting up from the bench, 'let's take a look at that shed.'

'What, now?' I protested.

'Can you think of a better time? Jeff's off out of it, so let's make the most of our opportunities. I'm game if you are.'

'You're the boss,' I said and followed him back to the motorcycle.

Tom stopped the bike outside Patel's and ducked into the doorway to keep out of sight, while I crept across to my house and down the side passage. Stranger than keeping a watch on your own house is to steal round it like a burglar. Tom had equipped me with a slender but hefty spanner, long enough to lever away the padlock and its fittings from the shed door. If my mother came out, I would make a dash for it across the gardens and disappear down someone else's side passage. I was intent on being quick and bold, but as the garden was quiet I couldn't resist the temptation to stop and stare at the house which was familiar but no longer seemed like my home. It was as if I'd been away for years.

A light was on in the kitchen. My mother was making a mug of cocoa. I watched her go back and forth across the empty room like counter staff in a chip shop after closing time; she looked bleak and lonely.

I watched from behind the dustbin as she shuffled towards me and locked the back door. A few moments later the light went out and the kitchen door gently closed.

I moved silently to the shed and made ready to use the spanner, but it was not needed. The lock dangled uselessly at an angle. Hovis had been here before me. No one else would have done this. The door had been pushed to so that the casual observer would never have noticed anything amiss, but it opened easily.

Inside, half the floor had been torn up. Hovis could have done this without any trouble if my mother had been round the front with the television turned up. I couldn't see very well, so I got down on my hands and knees and felt around the scattered planks and damp earth. I searched quickly but methodically, working from one side of the shed to the other. There was no obvious sign of a package or anything else Jeff might have hidden. But just inside the door my fingers found a strip of coarse paper. I grabbed it up carelessly and shoved it in my pocket like I would a sweet wrapper. I closed the door behind me and sprinted back up the path.

Tom was already sitting astride the bike by the time I reached him. He let out the throttle as I climbed on and we roared off; we raced away with our hearts pounding like two kids spotted scrumping apples in the rain.

Tom stopped along the main road into town. We were both cold, weary and very wet.

174

'What happened then?' he asked, out of breath.

'Nothing . . . Hovis beat me to it.'

'What took you so long? I nearly came looking.'

'Oh . . . my mum in the kitchen,' I said sadly. 'Then I had to search the shed, it was a hell of a mess. The floor had been ripped right up!'

Tom made no further comment. He was thinking I should have gone in and spoken to my mum, but he wasn't prepared to say so.

'You need a change of clothes,' he said. 'And what's more, it's about time I introduced you to the Missus.'

'Right,' I said, too tired to protest. Even though it was only half past ten, it had been a long day.

It was only a short journey to Tom's flat, but I was still very relieved when we'd finished climbing the stairs to the fourth floor.

Tom's missus opened the door to us with a smile so warm she could have set up as a solarium and charged people to look at her.

'Look at the state of you both!' she exclaimed, but not seeming the least bit surprised. 'Come in, come in. You'll catch your death of cold standing there.'

The Missus was a tiny woman, tanned as a walnut and twice as wrinkled. She led us into the sitting room and demanded our clothes. I didn't know where to put myself. She became a blur of movement and darting, nimble hands, and in no time at all we were both stood stark naked in front of the gas fire. Tom and me that is, not the Missus! As it was, I'd never been so embarrassed in all my life.

'Who's been feeding you?' she said, looking me up and down as if I was livestock at an auction. 'Looks like the birds have been getting more than their fair share of yours. Poor lad needs feeding up, doesn't he, Tom?'

175

Fortunately, at this point Tom came to my rescue with a towel, which felt as prickly as a horse blanket but was none the less welcome. The Missus made cocoa and sandwiches. We talked a lot, but where we'd been was never mentioned. Tom's missus was not a woman to pry into men's affairs, or so she kept telling me. She said she didn't have to, because she knew just the sorts of things they got up to. Whatever it was didn't matter, because it all resulted in the same dirty washing, just when you least wanted it.

The Missus chattered on and on. She out-talked Tom, and I couldn't keep up with it. She knew all about me, that was obvious, but she never said anything about it.

Tom was asleep in his chair when I got up to go. Not once had we had the opportunity to talk about the shed, apart from the brief account I had given him as we climbed the stairs to his flat. The Missus had lent me some old clothes, and I started towards the door looking like the ghost of jumblies past.

'And where do you thing you're going, young man?'

I hadn't anticipated this show of kindness. Any other time and I would have welcomed it. Tom's flat was cosy and homely, with its red plush wallpaper and horse brasses hanging over the gas fire, but I hadn't finished for the night. I was unsettled by the excitement of the evening's events, and as I had begun to recover from the cold my thoughts had grown restless. I was full of sandwiches and cocoa, but a craving still remained. All this cosiness just made me feel lonely, and I wanted to talk to Sharla.

'You've still not answered me, Wayne,' the Missus persisted. She had the only exit covered, and her arms were folded meaningfully across her chest.

'Ah . . . ' I began, and promptly stopped on the edge of a lie about how I didn't want to trouble her with putting me up for the night. The truth, I decided, was the only road to freedom.

'Yes?'

'I know it seems ridiculous, but I have to go and see a friend of mine,' I said.

'What, at this time of night? It's half past eleven. That's no time to be calling on a young lady, now is it, Wayne?'

How did she know? I was sure Tom would never have told her about Sharla.

'Then again,' she said with a fond smile, 'I do remember a certain young man, not too far from here, who used to get up to such things on occasions . . . And I could tell you a story about him and my father and the night he caught him with a branch snagged under his belt, dangling upside down from the pear tree outside my window. Today a young man doesn't have the opportunities for pleasure that we had then. That was before people regarded trees as useless and installed double glazing, which is something else I don't hold with . . .'

By the time she'd got to the word 'draught', as in 'it's not healthy to live without a good draught', she'd stood aside to let me pass.

'Thanks,' I said, as I made for the front door.

'Well, Tom came to no harm by it, so I imagine you'll come to none!' And then she called, 'Goodnight, dear, and don't forget to take that coat!'

I took the ancient raincoat off the hook in the hall, and when I'd closed the front door, I leapt down the stairs filled with a double dose of cheer and determination.

Chapter 15

Tom's flat was about half a mile from the railway station. I was safe from Hovis in this part of town, Jeff had more than enough to think about, and I was free to walk the streets without having to skulk in the shadows. All good things come to an end though, and when I reached the station I squeezed under the car-park fence where kids had hollowed out a passage, and set out on the three-mile walk down the line to Sharla's house.

By the time I reached the crossing by our estate, the rain had all but died. The wind washed everything in gentle drizzle. I stopped at the crossing and waited for ten minutes, watching and listening. When a fox crossed the rails a few yards away I was sure that all was clear.

Further on up the line the glasshouse stood tranquilly in the dark. I passed quietly by. The rain stopped. Silence fell. The late-night traffic had ceased. I plodded along the tracks in the direction of school.

When it came to it, Sharla's house was quite difficult to identify. From the back, all the houses along her road looked the same in the dark. Each one was pebble-dashed, with the identical clutter of drainpipes clinging to its walls, and each garden contained a similar collection of ramshackle sheds and untidy heaps of garden rubbish.

At intervals I would jump up and peer over the fence, and eventually I found what I was looking for, Sharla's guinea-pig hutch under the kitchen window. It was instantly recognizable. I had helped her paint it a bright purple at school in CDT.

The fence was six feet high and constructed of smooth, vertical wooden planks, making it difficult to climb. Regularly placed fence-posts protruded a few inches above the timbers. I took off the old raincoat, and hooked the collar over the nearest fence-post, tugging it hard to make sure it would stay secure when I put my weight on it. The coat was a tough old garment and already very well worn. I didn't think Tom or his missus would mind if I used it as a makeshift ladder. The pockets were ideal toe-holds, and I scaled the fence without too much difficulty. Clambering down the other side was no problem, because two bars ran horizontally between the posts.

Sharla's room was next to the bathroom at the back of the house, like mine. She'd complained about sleeping with her head next to the toilet often enough. I collected some lumps of mud from the foot of the fence, and crept down the garden path. The house was in darkness.

My first attempts at waking Sharla were unsuccessful. The mud was too soft, and simply spattered down from the window like rain on my head. Gravel was what I needed, but there was none around. I had to resort to small stones. The first one hit the window with a bang loud enough to wake the whole neighbourhood; the second punched a small hole in the glass. It all happened in slow motion, but there was nothing I could do to restore the situation. There was no way of playing the film backwards. The window had cracked from corner to corner.

Sharla screamed and screamed, and I fled in a panic back down the garden and scrambled over the fence. I crouched down on the other side, listening.

I could get a clear view of the scene through a crack

between the boards. Sharla's light came on first, followed shortly afterwards by the fluorescent tube in the kitchen. Then the back door opened and someone burst out into the garden. It was Sharla's dad, and he was hopping mad.

He headed straight down the path like a man making the first arrangements for a shot-gun wedding. He looked left and right, shining his torch into every nook and cranny. I pressed myself into a tight ball at the foot of the fence. Sharla's dad stopped only a few inches away from me on the other side of the planks. I could distinctly hear his heavy breath. The boards clattered in my ears; he was clambering up to have a look.

The torch searched up and down the tracks. Then it went off. I knew he was still there, quietly listening. I held my breath. The torch flashed on again, and once more played over the tracks and raked across the embankment. Fortunately for me, Sharla's dad never thought to look down at his own feet. Only a turnip-brain like me would think of staying rooted to the spot.

I began to wonder whether he would ever go away, but then Sharla's mum called him from the kitchen door.

'Come on in now, Jack, the girl's all right. You can't do anything more tonight.'

'Yeah, okay, love.' There was a reluctance in his voice. 'Have you called the police?'

He stepped off the fence and moved away.

'No, dear, I haven't,' she said. 'I can't go down to the box like this. What if anyone saw?'

'I'll go then.' There was a note of irritation in his voice. His step was heavy as he made his way back to the house.

'No, come back in,' his wife insisted. 'It can wait until

the morning. They won't do anything anyway. Whoever it was will be long gone by now.'

Then the door closed with a bang, and the kitchen light flickered off.

Sharla's light stayed on, and I hung around to see what was going to happen. Her dad appeared with some paper and tape, and began to make a rough repair to the broken pane. Then he pulled the curtains and the light went out.

As I got up to go, the light clicked on again, and then off.

I waited.

The light flashed on and off several times like a signal. Sharla had been doing some thinking. Who on earth would break her window at this time of night? She had thought she heard a faint rapping on the pane before, somewhere in her dream. Who would use this clumsy method of waking her up? Only a complete turnip-brain, and the only turnip-brain she knew was me.

I was back on top of the fence as she appeared at her window. I was excited. What an end to the day this was going to be!

By the time I stepped into the pool of light beneath her room, she had the window open.

'Wayne, is that you, you pillock?'

'Yes,' I whispered nervously.

'What are you doing here?'

'I've come to see you,' I said, as if it was the obvious thing to do at that time of night. 'I need to speak to you.'

'Brilliant!' she said sarcastically. 'Well, you'd better make it quick, or my dad'll be up again.'

'Yeah, right.' I was beginning to feel distinctly foolish. 'Sorry about the window.'

'For God's sake!' she hissed. 'You didn't do all this

damage just so you could apologize for it afterwards, did you? Get on with it. I'm getting cold.'

'No, look, I've run away from home. It's complicated. I need to explain.'

'What? Now?'

'No, tomorrow, stupid,' I said foolishly.

'Well, if you're going to stand there and insult me, I'll just shut this window now and call my dad!'

'No, no, don't do that! Please. Sorry, it's me who's stupid.'

'Look, I'll have to go.' Sharla was glancing over her shoulder, and there was a note of panic in her voice. 'Someone's up!'

The light went off, and I ducked down against the kitchen wall. The bathroom light came on. I heard a dull fart, and a gut-wrenching smell wafted out of the fan-ventilator. Then I got the giggles. The toilet flushed, which drowned out my spluttering, and the light went off again.

After a moment, Sharla's window opened again, but the light stayed off.

'You there?' came Sharla's voice in an exaggerated whisper.

'Yeah. Who was that?' My shoulders were still shaking.

'My mum. Why?'

'Nothing,' I said, biting my lip.

'What?' Sharla was beginning to sound exasperated.

'Nothing,' I repeated, getting a grip on myself at last.

'Nothing what? Oh, this is stupid!'

She was about to close the window, so I carried on quickly, before I had time to collapse into hysterics again.

'When can we talk?' I asked, hoping she would remain patient for a little while longer.

'Tomorrow. But only if you're going to be sensible.'

'Where?' I said.

'At school?' she suggested.

'No, I'm not going to school any more.' I said this calmly as if my decision was final and irreversible.

'What! You mean you're giving up?' Sharla sounded astonished. 'You can't do that!'

In a moment she would get into full flow and forget where she was and what time it was, as she endeavoured to sort me out.

'Look, I'll have to go in a minute,' I insisted. 'Your dad, remember? I'll meet you by the garage next to the scrapyard on the main road. Okay?'

'Yeah, all right, I'll see you tomorrow. What time?'

There was a noise from within the house, and Sharla began to close the window.

'Seven o'clock,' I whispered desperately. I wasn't sure whether she'd heard me.

I beat a retreat down the garden.

When I got back from Sharla's there were two men in Mrs Philpot's garden. They were doing something behind the glasshouse. I lay flat on the chippings by the railway line and watched. The men looked around as if they'd heard something. They were jumpy. I pressed my face hard against the sharp stones. Their faces looked familiar.

It was only when I saw Jeff come down the garden path that I finally realized who they were. But how could Jeff have discovered my whereabouts? And why had he brought his friends with him? He couldn't possibly have recognized me in my kamikaze outfit, and even if he had, he still wouldn't have known where to find me.

As Jeff neared the glasshouse, I could see that he was carrying a flat package under his arm. The package was

183

about three feet square. He obviously wasn't looking for me at all. But what was he doing at the glasshouse?

Unable to move without causing a disturbance, I lay helplessly on top of the embankment. Jeff joined the two men behind the glasshouse and set his package down. Then the most unexpected thing happened. Jeff unscrewed the downpipe, which drained rainwater from the roof of the glasshouse into a huge water-butt. The pipe came off easily. Then the three men put their weight behind the heavy barrel and began rotating it, so it moved slowly to one side. It revealed a dark circle underneath, which to me looked like the ordinary damp mark a water-butt would leave behind if moved.

Jeff put his arm into the water-butt and drew out a long T-shaped handle, which he inserted into the dark circle. He twisted the handle slowly and after three or four complete turns pulled it out. Then his two companions bent over the dark circle and pulled up a heavy metal lid, like a manhole cover, but ten times as thick.

Jeff disappeared into the earth with his package. His companions walked back along the garden path towards the house.

I was aghast at what I'd seen, not so much at Jeff and his friends, but at the revelation of this hole under the water-butt behind the glasshouse.

As the two men reached the door in the wall, I slithered quietly down the embankment to the fence. I could see the glasshouse just as clearly as when I'd first caught sight of it from this same position, but now everything was different. That had been only a week ago, but it seemed more like years. The two men returned to the hole behind the glasshouse with fresh loads.

Jeff seemed to get everywhere. It shocked me to think how he must have discovered the glasshouse before me, before I'd innocently made it my home. Without knowing it, I had stumbled on territory already claimed by the Hell Snakes of Steel. So much for revenge! Jeff had got the last laugh as usual. I was too weary and despondent to do anything but watch.

The unloading of the blue Transit, which I imagined was parked on the track outside Mrs Philpot's house, was done in silence, and only took half an hour.

The three men worked fast.

When they'd packed up and gone, I examined the area at the back of the glasshouse. The water-butt and down-pipe had been replaced. It was as if no one but myself had ever been there. I could have imagined it all, but when I dipped my hand into the water and felt the cold steel of the T-shaped handle, I knew that everything I had witnessed was real.

I put my weight against the butt. It was useless; I didn't have the strength to shift it, not even so much as an inch. I might as well have tried to move the glasshouse itself.

So I gave up and let myself into the glasshouse to get some sleep, though I lay awake for a long time, too disturbed by what I'd seen even to think about Sharla. I had come so far, and yet seemed to have got nowhere. Right now I was lying on top of God knows what sinister secret. There was more to Jeff's evil than I could ever have imagined, and Hovis was still out there waiting for me somewhere in the dark. I was at the heart of something mad, but hiding as I was down behind the staging in the glasshouse, I was at least safe for a while. Not even Sharla knew where I was.

Chapter 16

I awoke to a frantic banging on the glass, then the glass-house door sliding open. Bleary-eyed, I expected to see Tom, but instead there stood his missus.

'Before you start asking,' she began, 'Tom can't come, but he'll be all right. I won't let him out of bed this morning. He made such a fuss, saying he had to get here and the like. I said, "No, Tom, you stay here; I'll see to the boy." I had to lock him in. I've got both keys. Poor man, a prisoner in his own home. But it's for his own good. Gallivanting about the countryside like that, motorcycle-scrambling at his age. At night and all, and out in all weathers. Not to mention leading a young boy astray, which only makes it worse. How are you this morning, anyway? I hope you had a comfortable night?'

My head thumped like it was being dragged along behind a train.

'I'm fine, thanks,' I said feebly, clutching my blankets tightly around me in case the Missus had the idea of tipping me out. 'Is Tom really all right?'

'Yes, yes. But you stay where you are. I'll make you some breakfast. He's caught a cold, that's all. You've got to be careful when you're seventy-eight!'

'He said he was seventy-four,' I replied in astonishment.

'Ah, that's what he tells everybody. He reckons it goes down better with the girls. We have to humour him, don't we?'

'He's still quite tough though, isn't he?' I said.

'Aye, he'll last a few years yet, as long as that two-wheeled Bath chair of his keeps going!'

'Sorry?' I said.

'The Triumph. He cares more about that bike than anything else. You know he drags it up four flights of stairs just to clean it. The times I've fallen over it in the hall!'

The Missus prattled on merrily, and the events of the night before became more and more remote.

'Don't you think it's a bit funny,' I said at last, stuffing a bacon sandwich into my mouth and feeling a lot better, 'me not going to school and living here and all that?'

'None of my business,' was all she said in reply but then she added, 'I minds my own. By the way, I've washed your clothes. Which reminds me, Tom asked me to give you this, though God knows why, it's only a scrap of paper. He said you'd be interested in having it back. I found it in your pocket when I washed your trousers. Still, we have to humour him, don't we?'

'Yes, I suppose so,' I said, beginning to understand what she was on about.

'Well, here it is for what it's worth.'

The Missus handed me what she had referred to as a scrap of paper; it was in fact the torn-off top of a Jiffy bag. Two of the staples still remained, pinching the paper together where the bag had been sealed.

'Thanks,' I said. 'And thank Tom for me as well. I'd forgotten all about this.'

She looked at me curiously, as if to say that men were all just grubby little boys at heart and there was no point trying to understand them.

When she'd gone I took a closer look at the top of the Jiffy bag. It was just like the ones which had come through the

187

post for Jeff. But there was more than that, which was no doubt why Tom was so keen that I should have it back. Something was attached to the top, sandwiched tightly between the stapled fold of the envelope. It was a scrap of paper, smaller than a postage stamp, blue and white, with the letters 'on' printed on it in the smallest type. I recognized it as the torn corner of a £5 note.

Jeff had been receiving money through the post, and remembering the articulated feel of the package, I guessed it had been a lot of money. Somebody trusted the Post Office, but Jeff obviously didn't trust banks. What a muddle it all was. I'd got Hovis's money stashed away under the staging and Hovis had got Jeff's money, or at least that's what it seemed like. But what on earth was it of Jeff's that I was sitting on now? The hole under the shed had been small, but what of the hole under the glasshouse. How far did that extend?

I got up and put my proper clothes back on. I ached all over from the bike ride of the previous night. Saddle-sore wasn't in it; my bum felt like it had been tenderized with a steak hammer.

I went round to the back of the glasshouse again and felt in the water-butt. The handle was still there.

Waiting all day for Sharla was like waiting for Christmas. The more I thought about her, the further away from me she seemed. I was sitting in a glasshouse built on top of God knows what, and without Sharla's help I couldn't do anything about it. My only other friend, Tom, was stuck in bed for the time being, and anyway I reckoned he'd had enough excitement for a while.

I was as sure as I could be that Jeff wouldn't come back during the hours of daylight, and probably not until gone midnight, if at all. That would give Sharla and me plenty of time to try to shift the water-butt and take a look down the hole in the ground. I didn't think Tom would mind me bringing Sharla to the glasshouse in the circumstances. He was as keen as I was to unravel the mystery of Jeff's late-night antics.

By lunch-time, I was so racked with curiosity that I decided I'd try phoning Mrs Philpot from the call box on the main road. There were a lot of nursing homes in the phone book and I'd tried about five of them before I found one which would own up to having care of her. A rather curt voice at the other end of the phone explained that Mrs Philpot was engaged with a visitor, and that there was no way she could be brought to the phone. It was then that I ran out of money, and had to give up.

Never have I known a day to pass so slowly. I pottered around the glasshouse and must have readjusted the positions of hundreds of pots of dormant orchids.

I stoked the boiler and dampened the glasshouse floor.

By three o'clock, I'd finished the last of the sandwiches Tom's missus had brought over.

I was still four hours away from my meeting with Sharla, that is if she came, and I was beginning to have my doubts. I now wished I'd made the arrangements more clearly and set an earlier time for the meeting. I even wished I could be back at school. The glasshouse was a lonely place without Tom to brighten it up with his cheerful humour.

In desperation, I tried doing some press-ups as a gesture towards attaining super-hero status, but after three and a half I collapsed in a heap, absolutely knackered, my arms quivering like bow-strings. Headlines flipped through my head in rapid succession:

HAWKMASTER HAMMERS TATTOOED STRANGER
HAWKMASTER HAS HOVIS FOR BREAKFAST

HAWKMASTER IN HANG-GLIDING LOVE TANGLE:
'GET KNOTTED!' –
SHARLA'S HIGH-FLYING DENIAL
WIMP DECAPITATED IN CHEST EXPANDER TRAGEDY

And so the minutes dragged. I conjured up one fantasy after another, and in the end I have to admit that most of them were about getting off with Sharla.

Chapter 17

At six-thirty, I was hanging around in the alley between the scrapyard and the petrol station, out of sight just in case Jeff came by in the car. I must have counted every car which went past. I paced up and down. My hands sweated, I wished I'd cleaned my teeth; my glasses steamed up, my nails were grubby. I was a nightmare of personal hygiene; I was a derelict. Still, it's not looks but personality that counts, I told myself, but was not convinced. I didn't rate high in the personality stakes either.

At five to seven I heard Sharla's light step approaching. I inched to the end of the alley, close in to the scrapyard fence. As she passed me, I put my hand over her mouth and pulled her back into the shadows. She didn't even attempt to scream. Instead she elbowed me in the guts and put me on the floor before I had a chance to identify myself.

Then she was bending over me, not at all mad, having recognized me at last.

'Blimey, it works!' she exclaimed.

'What does?' I muttered through my teeth, clutching my stomach.

'Basic self-defence technique,' she said. 'A police-woman taught it to all the girls at the Youth Club. Pretty good, eh?'

'Yeah,' I gasped, and flopped against the fence.

'Are you all right, Wayne? You look a bit pale.'

'Yeah, brilliant,' I said. 'I'll be all right in a minute.'

Then, suddenly, Sharla was pulling at my arm and hauling me on to my feet fast.

'Come on, quick. Let's get a move on. Come on, Wayne, run!'

There was a new urgency in her voice, and I immediately saw why. Hovis's huge silhouette was looming at the end of the alley.

At first he couldn't locate us in the dark, and that gave us a couple of seconds' start. I grabbed Sharla's hand to pull her along, but she overtook me and dragged me skittering behind her down the alley.

She kept whispering, 'Which way? Which way?'

'Follow me,' I said, and overtook her as she slowed. I swung her round at the end of the alley like in a game of chain tag, and she found herself flung into a corner where the alley joins the track outside Mrs Philpot's house. I ducked in behind her, and as Hovis rushed on unaware of the geography of the place, I stuck my foot out up high and got him right in the goolies. Hovis doubled up.

We didn't hang about, and I towed Sharla off to the tunnel under the railway line.

'I couldn't have done better myself,' she said as we came out on the other side of the tracks. 'No one deserved his chances ruined more than Hovis!'

'There's no time to talk,' I said. 'Quick! Up here!'

We scrambled up the embankment and ran across the line above the tunnel. In no time at all we were in the garden, and safe from Hovis.

Sharla was quite amazed by the hidden garden. She too had no idea that it existed. I could see the words forming on her lips, but I put my fingers to her mouth, more gently this time. I led her round to the back of the glasshouse.

'Is this where you've been hiding?' she asked. 'Is this what you wanted to tell me about?'

'Yes, amongst other things,' I replied, rather too wistfully, as I began to unscrew the downpipe, just as Jeff had done the night before. I put the pipe on the ground while Sharla watched with a puzzled expression.

'What are you doing, Wayne?'

'No questions yet. Listen, grab the rim of the water-butt, and when I say twist, we'll try to rotate it. It's the only way of shifting it.'

'All right, if we must, but what's all the mystery?'

'No questions, remember?' I insisted. 'Now, twist!'

We put every ounce of our weight behind it, but we could hardly budge it at all.

'It's no good, you're not strong enough,' she said.

'Me?' I said. 'What about you?'

'Keep your hair on, Wayne, I didn't mean anything.'

We tried once again, but had no more success than the first time. It was too heavy.

'It would take three of us to shift that,' said Sharla as we flopped down and sat shoulder to shoulder with our backs to the water-butt. I began to enjoy this moment of closeness, but my pleasant thoughts were rudely interrupted. Someone had spoken, and it wasn't Sharla!

I looked round, startled, and got to my feet. Sharla rose slowly beside me.

'Well, fancy finding you here, Wayne. Your mother's been ever so worried about you. I told her I'd find you sooner or later, but I never expected to run across you here.' He paused, then added abruptly, 'And with your girlfriend!'

Sharla moved closer to me, and took my hand.

I looked at Jeff. He was standing at the corner of the glasshouse, between us and the scrapyard wall. Next to him was Hovis. He stooped slightly and was rubbing his groin. He didn't appear too happy.

'What's your friend's name again?' he persisted.

'I'm Sharla. What's it to you?' If looks could kill, Jeff would have been very dead.

'Leave her out of this, Jeff,' I said.

Jeff scowled. He was acting mean and hard in a way I hadn't seen before. Usually, he was fired up and mad as hell when he dealt with me at home, but now there was something cold and ruthless in his attitude. I didn't know how to deal with it.

'Hovis, tie their legs together, there's a good boy,' he said, pulling his belt from the waistband of his jeans. Hovis caught the belt cleanly, and advanced menacingly towards us. So they were in it together.

Jeff moved in closer, and Hovis tied Sharla and me by our legs like two kids in for the three-legged race. The coarse leather bit into my ankle painfully.

'Now,' said Jeff, when Hovis had finished, 'I'll show you how it's done. You don't need a third person. Cop hold of the rim, Hovis.'

Hovis pressed his bulk against the barrel.

'Right, twist, as our little friends would say.'

I didn't like the way he referred to us as 'little friends'. The contempt in his voice was crushing. Sharla was staying calm. I don't think she understood the enormity of what was happening.

Jeff and Hovis heaved the water-butt aside slowly but surely.

'There she goes,' said Jeff at last. 'What a beauty, eh?'

Hovis too was beginning to look puzzled, but a brain like his didn't take too much to confuse it.

'What you want, Wayne, is some muscles.'

There was an obscene edge to Jeff's voice. He pushed

up his sleeve and bared his tattoo. The steel snake stirred and rippled.

'Fancy these, do you, Sharla?' he continued, and patted her cheek. 'Maybe when you grow up a bit, eh? Hovis more your sort is he?'

Hovis grunted. Sharla tensed beside me, tight-lipped. I felt like booting Hovis in the balls again. Sharla must have been thinking along the same lines, because she could contain herself no longer and said, 'How's your goolies, Hovis?' Then she continued in a mocking voice, 'Which one's black, and which one's blue . . . or are they both a bit of each?'

Hovis made a move to thump Sharla, but Jeff held him back.

'Later, Hovis, later,' he said, with the same cold sneer in his voice. 'You'll get yours soon enough.'

Jeff was a nastier piece of work than I'd ever imagined. He was a big Hovis, but with fewer moral qualms and a presence which made Hovis seem a harmless cartoon character by comparison.

He had my mum fooled.

Then Jeff reached into the water-butt, and drew out the dripping T-bar. It glistened in the moonlight. He inserted it into the steel lid. After four turns he withdrew it, and stabbed it back into the water-butt with a hiss, like a yob stubbing out a cigarette in a pint of best bitter.

'Right, Hovis, when I say "when", you pull on these hand-holds here, see?'

'Yeah, I see 'em,' said Hovis. His brain flickered dimly as a thought struggled across its surface. 'What's down here, Jeff?'

'You'll see, soon enough. Just do as you're told. Ready?'

Hovis took up his position.

'When,' said Jeff, and Hovis heaved on the lid. It was a struggle at first, but then the lid began to swing up almost effortlessly under its own momentum. There must have been some mechanism to help him once he got it going.

'Right, Hovis, untie their legs. They won't be able to get through the hole otherwise. We don't want any accidents now, do we?'

Hovis fumbled at our ankles, eager to do Jeff's bidding. We looked down on him with total contempt. Jeff didn't seem to rate him too highly either, and he began to order him about again.

'Keep hold of them!' he snapped. 'Right, pass me the girl. She can go first.'

Sharla shot me a nervous glance, and I attempted to smile back at her reassuringly, as though I already knew the solution to our predicament.

'Right, my dear.' The way Jeff kept saying 'right' was beginning to get on my nerves. Maybe he was slightly on edge too. 'There's a switch on your left as you go in. Just flick it on will you?'

Sharla stepped into the hole, and just as suddenly the circle in the ground shone intensely silver, like a full moon. I watched Sharla's head disappear. I could see heavy concrete steps leading down into the cavity under the glasshouse.

'You next, Wayne,' Jeff ordered. 'Then Hovis. Then me.'

Hovis shoved me towards the hole. He dug his nails into my neck painfully.

'Gently, gently,' crooned Jeff. 'Don't damage the goods.'

The light was blinding after the darkness above. Sharla was at the foot of the steps, looking around with a puzzled expression on her face. I joined her, and instinctively put my arm around her shoulder and pulled her close. She didn't move away.

The place was beyond belief. It was like an enormous concrete tomb, running the length and breadth of the glasshouse. At the far end there was a huge steel door set in the wall. Next to it was a full set of kitchen units with a cooker, twin-tub washing machine and fridge. None of which were modern, but they had obviously never been used.

Along half of one side wall were eight wooden bunks, in pairs. The bunks were bare. No one had ever slept in them. The mattresses were still sealed in plastic wrappers. The remainder of the wall was occupied by shelves and cupboards. Everything you would ever need in a home was there in this strange cellar. It was like a vast concrete caravan, or boat. Or submarine. It was a complete subterranean home. There was even a small desk, a sofa and a reading lamp.

On the wall there hung watercolour paintings of orchids, and photographs of an old man, who must have been Alice Philpot's father. There was also a sepia photograph of a young man standing by an ancient tractor. He looked like a racing driver. It was Alice Philpot's husband, Billy. On the desk was another photograph, in a silver frame. It was Tom, with his Triumph. The Triumph sparkled. The picture had been taken when the bike was brand-new.

Oddly, the room was warm and dry. Large pipes ran across the ceiling of the room.

'What is it?' Sharla asked as she led me further into the room. 'And what are these?'

There were boxes and sealed packets all over the floor, like the ones I'd seen the night before at the house in the country, and like the ones the three men had carried down the garden path from the pale blue Transit.

'They're mine,' said Jeff proudly, coming up behind us. 'Tie their legs again, Hovis.'

Jeff was ordering Hovis about as if he owned him. Hovis obeyed like a dog.

'What is this place?' Sharla asked again, as Hovis tied our legs together.

'My bunker!' Jeff was beginning to sound like the Führer himself. 'Wonderful, isn't it?'

I protested, my voice straining with hurt and outrage.

'It's not yours!' I screamed. 'It belongs to –'

Jeff cut me off.

'So you're acquainted with the old biddy? I did a little removal job for her a while back and found the plans of all this. Her little secret, I reckon; even the old boy who looks after upstairs doesn't seem to know about it. She's as mad as a hatter, building this place.'

'No, she's –' I stopped myself just in time, before I gave away the secret of the project. I could at least try to save that. Jeff obviously didn't know what went on above, though he did know Mrs Philpot.

'What is all this?' Sharla broke in, her voice growing tense and showing signs of fear for the first time. 'You're just having us on aren't you, Mr Smith? I don't get what's happening. Why have you got us tied up? I know you and Wayne have had a bit of trouble recently, but all this is a bit sick isn't it?'

'What, darling, feeling sick are you? I think things are going very well, myself. What do you think, Hovis?'

'Yeah, great, Jeff,' Hovis replied, without much enthusiasm, and beginning to sound decidedly uneasy himself.

'And Wayne, what do you think of it?' Jeff went on. 'Better than home isn't it?'

I didn't answer. How could he say such things?

'Well, if you won't honour us with your views, then you can tell us what you and your friend are doing here in the first place?'

Jeff nudged me menacingly.

'Avoiding you … and him,' I snarled, gesturing towards Hovis.

'Shame you two don't get on,' said Jeff, with heavy sarcasm. 'Now let's all get comfortable. You two, sit down on the sofa over there, just like a proper little courting couple. We'll have some fun. We'll have a little quiz. I get to ask the first question, right?'

Sharla and I hobbled over to the sofa and sat down. I held her closer.

'Nice couple, aren't they, Hovis?'

Hovis made a move to sit down at the desk.

'I didn't give you permission to sit, Hovis. You can have a little lie-down later.'

Hovis cringed and backed off.

'Right, question numero uno: have you been following me, Wayne?'

Jeff paced up and down like a Gestapo interrogator. 'Well, have you?'

I shook my head.

'That right, Sharla?' he asked. 'Your four-eyed friend telling the truth?'

'Look, leave her out of this! Okay?' I screamed.

'That's nice, Wayne. Nice to see you sticking up for your friend. Well, Sharla, has he?'

She shook her head.

'Well then, Wayne, if you haven't been following me, how do you know about this little place? And who else knows?'

Jeff came over to me and glowered into my face. His breath smelt of beer and curry.

'I saw you last night on one of my walks,' I said.

'You were out late then.' He was considering my answer. It wasn't a lie. 'Where did you sleep? Where've you been staying?'

Jeff backed away into the middle of the room and sat down on a small crate.

'I've been at a friend's.' Once again I wasn't lying, but then I was forced into a fib. 'I couldn't sleep last night. I was worried about Mum.' I could feel my voice begin to shake. Sharla squeezed my hand. 'So I went for a walk along the railway line. That's how I stumbled on this place.'

'That may or may not be true.' I couldn't tell whether Jeff was convinced or not, but then he rounded on me savagely. 'Who else knows?'

'Nobody,' I said, 'honest!'

But he wasn't going to let the interrogation drop yet. 'Now, let's get something else straight. Why did you come here tonight?'

Sharla stepped in. 'We just ran in here. Hovis was after us. He must have been following me. He's been after Wayne for ages; he won't leave him alone.'

So that was how Hovis found me.

I should have guessed. Having lost me, he'd decided to watch Sharla in the hope she'd lead him to me. Quite clever for Hovis.

Sharla continued her version of events.

'Then we ran round here. Wayne said it would be a good place to hide, safe from that pillock over there. That's when he told me about the water-butt, that we might as well have a look while we were here. We were going back to his friend's caravan. We didn't mean to come in here. You know what a coward Wayne is, don't you? Think he'd go looking for trouble?'

Sharla sounded convincing. Even I began to believe it. She'd got some of her composure back.

Jeff thought about what she'd said. For a minute or so he stared at us cruelly, waiting for us to crack.

At last he broke the silence. 'Knowing you, Wayne, what she says could well be true. Is that right, Hovis? You followed her?'

'Yeah,' Hovis grunted, 'then I lost them outside the house when they tripped me up. He's still got something I want.' He made a move towards me, but Jeff's look held him back.

'Bit careless of you, eh, Hovis?'

Suddenly, Jeff smiled, the fake smile of a game-show host. He put his hands in his pockets and visibly relaxed. He got up and moved to the side of the room.

'Now, fair's fair. I've had my turn. It's your go now, Wayne. I can see from your freckled little four-eyed face that you're just dying to ask me something. Fire away. I'm all ears.'

Jeff awaited my reply. I thought for a moment. What I wanted to know was, why Jeff had turned up in the garden with Hovis, if Hovis had been following Sharla, and then chasing the two of us. How come Jeff had arrived on the scene?

'Speed it up!' said Jeff. 'You have to miss a go if you dawdle about. Come on. Ten seconds. One . . . two . . . three . . .'

'Well,' I said, 'what are you doing here with Hovis? I mean, it's a bit off, you knocking around with a kid from my school –'

Hovis interrupted. 'Piece of piss!' he said. 'I ran into Jeff outside the house and we made a deal. We've been doing business together for some time, ever since I met him on work experience. Jeff and me are partners, thanks to my friend Crease.'

'What? You're joking!' I shouted in disbelief.

'No bull,' said Hovis, looking pleased with himself.

'So you met up tonight by coincidence then?' I wasn't at all convinced.

The whole time Hovis was talking Jeff had been leaning against the bunk-beds, smirking and manicuring his nails with what I took to be a long thin paper-knife.

'Partners. That's right, ain't it, Jeff?' Hovis was seeking reassurance.

'Is it?' Jeff replied, pushing himself away from the bunks, and moving menacingly close to Hovis. The knife flashed in his hand.

'Is it?' he repeated.

Hovis backed away.

Jeff was no longer so relaxed. Something was erupting from deep inside him; something which had been simmering for a long time.

He matched Hovis step for step.

'Do you really think we met by chance?' Jeff's voice took on a cruel, cold, slow rhythm. 'Just how thick are you? I always thought Wayne was dim, but you take the biscuit!'

The knife danced beneath Hovis's throat.

'What's going on?' Hovis was suddenly very pale. He could imagine his blood on that cold concrete floor.

The steel blade flashed again and nicked a small hole in his jacket.

'Wayne, do something!' Hovis screamed. 'For Christ's sake do something!'

'Jeff,' I pleaded, 'come on, this isn't funny any more.'

It hadn't been funny for a long time.

'You shut up!' Jeff snapped, never taking his eye from Hovis for a single moment. 'This snivelling bastard has been trying to blackmail me. He's been poking his nose

202

into my private business. Lazy toad that he is, hanging around the depot one day, having a sly drag behind a stack of packing cases, Hovis hears a conversation between me and my mate about a job we just done. Hovis here thinks he's the Big Man, and starts making demands. So I strings him along for safety's sake, biding my time, giving him just enough to keep his trap shut. Then Hovis has to get greedy and wants a bigger cut. But £250 is more than I'm prepared to stand. On top of that, not only has he been sniffing around the shed looking for more, he's had the brass to rip up the floor and steal – you hear me Hovis? – steal what's mine. Big Boy here thinks he's entitled to a cut of my business! Grow up, Hovis, you're not nicking toffees from the likes of Wayne and his first year friends.'

Hovis had backed against the steel door at the end of the room and had nowhere to hide. Jeff put the knife to his throat.

'I've been watching you, son, just waiting for my opportunity. While you were following the pretty girl here, I was following you, but you were just too dumb to see.'

The blade twitched, and a drop of blood appeared under Hovis's chin.

'Lay off, Jeff!' I shouted. 'You've scared him enough. Leave him be can't you.'

'Shut up,' Jeff hissed, trying to control himself. He was trembling with rage. 'Shut up. I won't tell you again.'

Jeff edged sideways so he could see all three of us.

'Now, Hovis, where've you put my money?'

Hovis was too terrified to speak.

'Did you hear me?' Jeff spoke very slowly, each word like one twist of the water-butt. 'Open the door!'

Hovis pulled on the heavy handle. The door swung

back smoothly. It was several inches thick. Sharla and I stared open-mouthed at the walk-in freezer.

'You can cool off a bit, Hovis, then we'll see who'll talk.'

Hovis was about to plead, but the immediate fear of the knife shut him up and drove him backwards into the freezer. Jeff slammed the door with a flourish. He was enjoying himself.

The last I saw of Hovis was an appealing little-boy-lost look on his evil face. I actually felt sorry for him. Sharla buried her face in her hands.

Jeff turned to us, as if what we'd just witnessed was quite normal.

'Next question!' he said, like the mad quiz-master he had become. 'Sharla. Your turn.'

Sharla didn't look up. She didn't answer.

'Right, my turn again, then,' he crooned. 'And my next question is, what am I going to do with you two? Wayne, you're just a missing schoolboy, or you will be when your mum goes to the police tomorrow. And, well, Sharla, when you don't turn up, I reckon they'll work out that you two ran away together, particularly when I put my oar in about it. I'll have the whole town talking about your sordid romance . . .'

I had fallen under the spell of Mrs Philpot's dream, whatever this bunker had to do with it, only to see it turn into a nightmare. It was clear that Sharla and me were finished. There was small consolation in the knowledge that Tom could go to the police and do for Jeff, but it was too late for me and Sharla. It was the end of my happy dream, at any rate, and as if to emphasize the fact there was a distant rumbling overhead.

Jeff heard it first. Then Sharla looked up. The noise grew louder. It echoed down through the entrance hole and was amplified by the acoustics of the bunker itself. I thought of Tom's motorbike, but it couldn't be that. It was too loud, too powerful.

Jeff froze. He listened, absolutely motionless except for his face, which twitched. His rage was turning to panic. He didn't understand either, but his instinct told him to flee. He trusted no one, and was not to be trusted. There were plenty of others like him out there in his world, people who might try anything, and he wasn't about to be trapped underground by the likes of them. An animal sense of self-preservation was what drove him up the stairs and out through the hole into the garden.

Sharla thought more quickly than me. As soon as Jeff was half-way up the stairs, she was scrabbling at the buckle of the belt which wound our ankles together. Fortunately, Hovis was a lousy Boy Scout and she soon got us free.

Then there was an almighty crash like a building collapsing.

'Run, Wayne!' Sharla instructed me, and pushed me towards the stairs.

When I surfaced, I couldn't see Jeff. To my relief, the glasshouse was still standing. But the night was filled with noise, and what was on the way was terrifying.

It had come through the garden wall, scattering bricks everywhere. It had already destroyed the herbaceous border, and now its caterpillar tracks were tearing up the lawn. The machine lurched dangerously, its great electro-magnet swinging menacingly at the end of a mighty chain and system of heavy-duty cables. Jarvis's machine was lumbering straight towards the glasshouse. Its dark and demonic silhouette was unmistakable against the night sky.

Then Jeff was upon me, out of nowhere, and I was bundled to the ground. But in the darkness and confusion I wriggled free. He lost his footing on the slippery grass and I ran towards the machine. I stood before it, not knowing what to do next, all the while aware that Jeff was right behind me. For a moment, it was as if by standing still I could make the whole world stop with me, as if I could hold the machine at bay with a dramatic gesture of powerful wings. But I had no wings and the machine and Jeff kept coming on. Jarvis's monster was rumbling slowly, but inexorably, towards all the glass and all those years of work. I didn't know how to stop it, and there was no one to appeal to. There was no one in control of it; the driver's seat was empty.

Looming behind me, Jeff forced me closer to the grinding caterpillar tracks. There was no escape in just running, so I moved nearer to meet the machine on its own terms. I danced around it.

Jeff was now on the opposite side of the machine. We were like father and son, chasing each other around the trunk of a tree, except this was not a happy family game, and both Jeff and the machine were totally out of control.

I felt like I did when I got lumbered with playing in goal, and Wilkes bore down on me and all the girls were watching from the hockey pitch. I could try lunging, but it would be hopeless. I would lose the ball, while Wilkes trampled over me to the sound of distant laughter and the whistle blowing yet again.

Jeff and I couldn't go on circling the machine for ever.

I leapt when I least expected it. I thought of Sharla. Then Jeff was round my side of the mad machine and I made my lunge. Jeff mistimed his tackle and fell. I hit the steps beneath the driver's seat, and grasped the rail. As the machine lurched sideways, I hung on. The great steel tracks ground round and round, spitting up divots of earth, threatening to suck my feet in and mash them up. Beneath the noise, I imagined I heard a scream.

Then I clambered up and took possession of the seat. I couldn't see Jeff now, but the glasshouse was looming closer. A bewildering array of levers confronted me. It was impossible to find the fuel cut-off in the dark. I yanked at the nearest lever, and the machine swerved sideways. I pulled another and the magnet descended. I pulled it back and the magnet rose. The machine closed on the fragile wall of glass. I pulled the first lever again and held it hard. The machine lurched violently. It lurched all the way round. I felt suffocated and nauseated by the exhaust.

When I let the lever go, Jarvis's machine was lumbering away from the glasshouse in the direction from which it had come. I stood up in the seat, steadied myself, held my breath and then hurled myself as far as my strength would allow. A second later I was sprawled headlong in the mud. The ground was cold. It was good to be still. I was exhausted and drained. For a while I lay on my back and stared up into the darkness. Jarvis's machine seemed far away. It seemed even the earth had stopped revolving.

Then Sharla was pulling me up and slipping her arm through mine. I felt a flush of pride, as we watched the machine rumble further and further from us.

'Brilliant!' she said excitedly. 'You were brilliant. Wait till I tell them at school!'

'What? You saw it?' I said.

'Not everything. Just the last bit; you were brilliant.'

'You mustn't tell anybody . . .' I said, but my voice trailed away.

I had noticed a small mound on the grass. It was very

still and indistinct, but I knew that the heap was Jeff.

'What is it, Wayne?' said Sharla.

She still hadn't seen the heap.

'I think it's Jeff,' I said trying to stop my voice from splintering into brittle shards of glass.

'Sorry?' asked Sharla, who hadn't caught my drift.

'Over there.' I pointed across the garden. 'I think it's Jeff.'

She didn't have time to reply, because at that moment the machine, which had been shuddering and snorting back to the scrapyard all the while, crushed Jarvis's caravan. The crunch of bent aluminium and shattered plywood seemed to tear the night in two.

I could have taken satisfaction in that, but I couldn't remove my eyes from the motionless heap in the garden, the heap which was what was left of Jeff.

'I think I've killed Jeff,' I said. My voice quivered and shattered.

'Stay here,' said Sharla. Her voice was shaking, but she went. She crossed the garden with the strained assurance of someone about to examine an unexploded bomb.

As she reached Jeff's crumpled form, a blue light began to flash on the main road. I noticed a new silence. The traffic and the machine had stopped.

When I reached Sharla, her nerve had broken and she was being sick.

I turned away too. Jeff's leg below the knee had entirely gone and bone was poking out of the other. He was unconscious. I couldn't have coped if it hadn't been dark. The silence was short-lived. All at once there were two blue lights, circling, and a lot of noise coming from the road. Then the door at the top of the garden crashed open and in roared Tom, the headlamp of the Triumph cutting a course across the lawn.

I shut my eyes when the beam lit up Jeff.

Tom slipped the bike into neutral and let the engine idle. Then he climbed out of the saddle, to reveal his missus firmly perched on the pillion.

'Hurry, love,' he ordered. 'Fetch the police quick. They're not helping much out there.'

The Missus nodded and shuffled forward in the saddle, took hold of the handlebars, gripped the throttle, tripped the gears and roared off across the herbaceous border. She manoeuvred the bike through the gap in the wall and speedily negotiated the heaps of junk in the scrapyard.

'Move over quick, son,' Tom shouted above all the noise and confusion, 'and look to the girl. Take her off aways!'

I took hold of Sharla and led her back towards the glasshouse. I sat her down by the water-butt and from there I watched and waited, comforting her as best I could.

Tom was bending over Jeff and doing something to his legs. He worked quickly as though he knew exactly what he was doing, as though he'd done this kind of thing before.

The clamour on the main road died down and the powerful beam of car headlights cut through the scrapyard and stopped at the broken wall, picking out Tom who waved frantically into the light from where he was kneeling over Jeff.

The blue police lights flashed hypnotically, casting an eerie spell over the lawn and the piles of broken cars and twisted metal in the scrapyard. Then a searchlight electrified the garden and bounced back off the glass house. Two policemen came forward, hurrying towards Tom and Jeff. Just as they got close an ambulance arrived.

Radios buzzed; there was shouting. Sharla had still said nothing. I held her tight against me, in the shelter of the water-butt. A train roared past, its wheels wailing and then whispering into the distance. The radios crackled and went silent. Tom came back to us and Jeff was eased on to a stretcher and carried to the ambulance. Its siren blared and it was gone. A third set of blue lights glided into the scrapyard. Tom's face and Sharla's flashed from blue to white to blue to white to blue to white . . .

Chapter 18

We sat in the glasshouse. Over and over again, between asking me whether I was all right, Tom expressed his amazement at the discovery of the bunker; all that time he had worked there, he had no idea. He didn't know whether to be excited by the discovery or offended that Mrs Philpot had never let him into her final secret. There were endless questions to be answered. Tom had a few right now for Mrs Philpot, and he went off to phone her.

Sharla's father arrived to take her home. She was still in shock. Wrapped in a grey hospital blanket, she left the glasshouse silently, helped by her father and a WPC. She was to be interviewed at home, but she didn't have much to add to what the police had seen for themselves when they arrived in the garden.

I sat with the Missus at the far end of the glasshouse, in the company of Carlos, a detective-sergeant, and a social worker who had been called in to look after me while my mother was informed about Jeff.

We drank sweet tea, but it didn't taste like it usually does. I was cold and pulled my grey blanket tight round my shoulders. I was shivering, despite the warmth of the glasshouse.

Tom's missus filled me in on her part of the story. 'I only dropped off for a couple of minutes and all,' she said, 'but it's lucky I did. Otherwise Tom wouldn't have managed to get away and make his usual call to Mrs Philpot, and he'd never have known about the row she'd had with Jarvis. Of course he had to dash down here right away to check things were in order. Mind you, I insisted on coming along this time. Tom's not quite the young lad he thinks he is.'

It transpired that when I had phoned Mrs Philpot that afternoon, and was told by the snotty nurse that she was engaged with a visitor, that visitor had been Jarvis. He had been pushing his luck and making assumptions about the land he wanted to buy. His big mistake was to announce that he thought it was about time that the old greenhouse came down anyway. Mrs Philpot went bananas and tried to run him over in the electric wheelchair she used during her relapses. She had to be put back to bed and sedated, but not before she had screamed at Jarvis:

'I'll never sell, I'll never sell to you, Jarvis!'

And so it seemed Jarvis had set his machine loose, before beating a hasty retreat. No doubt he thought that if he destroyed the glasshouse, then Mrs Philpot would have no reason for not selling. But all he'd gained in the end was one squashed caravan.

When Tom returned he was full of news and extremely animated, far too excited even to drink his tea, which he left to cool on the staging while he talked. His story came pouring out. He'd extracted the truth from Alice Philpot at last.

The shelter under the glasshouse, he told us, had been the cause of all Alice Philpot's financial troubles and the reason for the reluctant sale of the orchard to old Mr Jarvis. The construction of a nuclear fall-out shelter was a lonely woman's plan to save her beloved orchids from the atomic bomb, which she had believed would drop at any time. She had planned for everything, except that the shelter would never be needed. A huge sum of money was wasted. Perhaps out of shame for her foolishness, she had kept the whole thing a dark secret all those years. But when Tom had told her over the phone about the drama in the garden she had owned up at once. In the circumstances, Tom had thought it best to leave well alone and not give her a piece of his mind.

All the while we sat and talked, policemen swarmed around and under the glasshouse. Tom had persuaded them that there was nothing within the glasshouse itself for them to see, and fortunately they left the plants undisturbed. Meanwhile, the detective-sergeant busily recorded everything I had to say. His questions were gentle, but penetrating. He got the story quickly. Apparently, a number of things he'd been working on were beginning to slot into place, and he talked about getting some unsolved crimes cleared up. My own story simply filled in parts of an emerging pattern. Jeff, he explained, seemed to be part of a gang who broke into large properties. They probably did it to order. The details would be arranged during meetings on motorway service stations and other inconspicuous places. Jeff would receive instructions and information. He would be told what to steal and where to find it. The people he worked for were probably faceless men in business suits, outwardly respectable citizens, who shipped the stuff overseas.

Jeff would do the dirty work. He stole paintings and jewellery mostly. Then, if the sergeant's hunch was right, he would deliver the goods in his firm's removal van to drop-off points conveniently close to his regular jobs. After all, shifting people's worldly goods about the country was his business, and one he carried out as if he was the most trustworthy man in the world. Nobody would ever lose a thing when Jeff was in charge of the van. Honesty was his cover. And his firm need never know about his illegal cargoes.

Jeff would be paid a retainer to keep him sweet between country-house jobs. When he delivered the stolen items and they'd been valued, his payment from the organization would come through the post from a series of fictitious business addresses. This explained the Jiffy bags I had told the sergeant about, that Jeff would hide in the hole under the shed, until he could split the money with his two mates, though he was probably fiddling them too.

I listened intently as the sergeant explained things. Then I told him about Hovis's connection with Jeff, and I'm afraid at that point I had to surrender the £250 Hovis had dropped in the precinct.

'And what about Hovis?' asked Tom, putting his arm round my shoulders, still concerned about my safety.

'No sign yet, I'm afraid,' said the sergeant. 'When your friend Sharla let him out of the freezer he took his opportunity in all the confusion and scarpered. No one's seen him since, but we'll get him before long. The description has gone out. I don't think there's too much to worry about there.'

At the end of it all, I sat with the Missus while Tom, the detective-sergeant and the social worker conferred in hushed voices.

The detective-sergeant went out into the garden, and it was the social worker who spoke to me next. She was a pleasant lady, not motherly, but big-sisterly.

'Well, Wayne, we'd better get you away from here,' she said.

Tom looked on. He was tired, but it was concern for me rather than fatigue which lined his face.

'Sergeant Williams has just gone off to find out what's

been happening with your mother and your stepfather. When he comes back, we'll know a bit more about where we stand.'

Tom smiled.

'Don't worry, Wayne, me and the Missus will see you right.'

The Missus nodded reassuringly and said, 'You're welcome any time, but right now I imagine you'll want to be back with your mother and little sister.'

'Yes,' I said. 'Thanks anyway.'

Then Sergeant Williams reappeared. The social worker went up the aisle to meet him. They consulted for a moment, exchanged smiles, and then returned together.

'Right then, Wayne,' said Sergeant Williams, in a tone of voice which suggested that things were never quite as black as they looked. 'I've been on the radio, and they tell me your mum is expecting you. You'll find WPC Adams is there helping to get things sorted out. Michelle . . . Miss Cheever here will take you back and she'll stay with you for as long as you and she see fit. Okay?'

So far, no one had said anything more about Jeff's condition. He had been alive when they'd taken him away. Tom had stemmed the flow of blood in the nick of time, and I was relieved about that. As much as I hated Jeff and feared him, and as much as I wanted revenge on him, all this super-hero stuff was only fantasy, and I didn't really want him dead. Seeing him on the ground, crushed by Jarvis's machine, had put things in a very new light. Really he was more to be pitied than anything else; just a maladjusted creep with a snake tattoo on his arm. I asked Sergeant Williams about him.

'It's touch and go,' he replied. 'He's in intensive care right now. The hospital says he's critical.'

I imagined Jeff in an oxygen tent, looking strange and

215

pale and small. I saw him plugged into machines, with plastic tubes stuck up his nose. I could hear the electronic blips and the hiss of gas. He was a powerless figure; the tattoo on his arm was merely fading ink etched into slack and grimy skin.

We walked through the scrapyard towards the main road: Tom, the Missus, Miss Cheever and me. Tom and his missus accompanied us as far as the Triumph, which she'd parked by the remains of Jarvis's caravan. The ground around was littered with torn magazines. I didn't have time to get a close look because I was quickly ushered on. A policeman was scuttling about picking them up and collecting them in a bin liner. He had already filled three by the looks of it. There was something in those magazines which they didn't want me to see, but I had a good idea what it was and knew that Jarvis was bound to get done for it as well as for everything else.

I barely had time to say my goodbyes to Tom and the Missus. Miss Cheever's car was parked up on the kerb. The traffic was flowing freely again along the main road. There was a lot of noise coming from the field opposite the scrapyard where an enormous recovery vehicle was trying to haul Jarvis's machine from where it had finally come to rest in the canal. Fortunately, nobody had been injured as it rumbled pilotlessly across the road.

As Miss Cheever unlocked the passenger door for me, Tom and the Missus sailed past. Tom beeped his horn and zig-zagged wildly, and then they disappeared towards town.

'You must be tired,' said Miss Cheever as she started the car and pulled away from the kerb.

I sank back into the seat and didn't say anything.

*

Miss Cheever was very nice to my mother when we got into the house. And I was glad to get inside. As we stepped out of the car I couldn't help but look around, in case Hovis was amongst the small group of nosy neighbours gathered at our gate. I rushed inside like a politician fearing imminent assassination.

WPC Adams had come to the door. She was the smallest policewoman I had ever seen and clutched her hat nervously, like a newly qualified air hostess who'd just realized she was scared of flying, and didn't dare tell anyone. She was obviously relieved to see us.

My mother was sitting on the sofa in the lounge with Ginny on her knee. It was way past Ginny's bedtime and she was red-eyed and miserable. My mother had kept her up for company. The television flickered silently in the corner of the room.

When we entered the lounge my mum didn't get up to greet me or scold me for running away from home, nor did she berate me about how worried she had been. She just looked defeated.

I didn't say anything, not even to Ginny. I flopped down in Jeff's armchair to stare miserably at the silent telly, while Miss Cheever did all the talking.

WPC Adams stood quietly in the doorway, turning her hat slowly round and round in her hands. She seemed embarrassed by the heavy footfalls of the policemen searching my mother's bedroom overhead. A spotlight had been rigged up in the garden and other policemen were rummaging through what Hovis had left of the shed.

Miss Cheever settled on the sofa next to my mother. Ginny buried her face in my mother's lank hair. It needed washing.

I should have felt triumphant in possession of Jeff's

chair, but I didn't. It just felt too big, like a hand-me-down jumper all stretched out of shape and smelling unfamiliar.

The silent advertisements flickering across the television looked contrived and crudely pasted together. Miss Cheever's voice sounded distant and hollow, like an overheard telephone conversation. I wasn't sure whether I ought to listen.

Questions turned themselves over in my mind. What now? remained unmoving at the centre. Everything else revolved around that.

What would my mum do about Jeff? What questions of loyalty and guilt were stirring within her? I couldn't read her face. She too was somehow disconnected from Miss Cheever's conversation. Would she stick by her broken husband, if he lived? God knows I didn't want to bear the responsibility for his death. Would he come back into our shattered household, or be gone for good? Where did I fit into my mum's life now?

I shuddered, and looked at Miss Cheever for reassurance. But she was too preoccupied with my mother to notice.

It seemed to me only Sharla, Tom and the glasshouse offered real hope for a brighter future. There was still a job to do with the orchids, and maybe we could all muck in together.

My idle dreams mingled with the unresolved questions floating around my head. I felt less alone.

Friends had begun to exert an influence on my life and I couldn't say I was sorry, having been in isolation for so long. Thanks to them, I had become a tougher kid, and some of my dreams now looked more attainable. With a bit of luck, and if I could keep Hovis at bay, things could only get better.